# WEALTH *of* DECEPTION

## HARRIET SPERLING FELTMAN

PAGE PUBLISHING, INC.
Conneaut Lake, PA

First originally published by Page Publishing 2020

All of the fictitious names, characters, events, and personal portrayals within this novel were written by the sole imagination of the author.

ISBN 978-1-64701-266-3 (pbk)
ISBN 978-1-64701-267-0 (digital)

Printed in the United States of America

I want to dedicate this book to my best friend, Jingles.
Her untimely passing at 61, taught me
to cherish every day.
Lung cancer is a killer.

# Chapter 1

Katherine was so proud of herself. She worked so hard at getting what she wanted. She was always trying to accomplish too much. Something within her made her work far beyond her own expectations. Katherine came so far and didn't want to let go. Her mind traveled back three weeks ago when she and Jonathan were together. She wanted a repeat performance. She was now in her car driving when she realized that the pain in her lower back was moving down into her right leg. She thought that it had to be from that ridiculous antique chair she bought for her desk. She would have to change it again. Yet, at the same time she giggled out loud to herself and the back pain went away as her mind remembered the man she was in love with. Oh, yes, she remembered all too well. She had to have his touches, his kisses, and of course, his bodily fluids smothering her own. She was now longing for his powerful arms around her, giving her the sense of heaven. She was driving faster and faster to keep their meeting. Nothing was going to keep her from him, not even the pain in her back.

It was those times, those moments that kept her going from day to day and week to week. Now it was time to make new memories. She didn't want to be late.

Jonathan made arrangements to meet at their regular place. His wife, Samantha, of ten years was always questioning him, "Where are you going tonight, Jonathan?" Samantha had some idea that he had someone else in his life. Katherine and Jonathan had to be very careful. Their usual rendezvous at the Inn of Nine Houses was going to be a special evening since it was one year from their first encounter.

When she arrived at the inn, Katherine raced into the bungalow. Jonathan had candles lit and her favorite music playing. The room was filled with warmth from the dozens of roses lining the room in fancy vases. Vases filled with all long-stemmed red roses, others filled with all yellow ones. There were baby's breath roses and tea roses. Roses were everywhere. Her heart was filled with love for this man.

As she entered the bathroom, she began to cry. She was so overwhelmed by his thoughtfulness. Candles were floating in the perfumed bathwater. On the counter were two small red roses taped to a small package with pink ribbons. She picked up her present, opened it, and again, had trouble holding back the tears. She had never seen such a beautiful necklace and matching bracelet. They were pearls with a hint of pink to them. She remembered that her grandmother told her that pearls were worn as a healing power. She loved them and put them on for her Jonathan.

His magnificent body was lying under a handcrafted afghan. "Come here. I've missed you. I can't stand not being with you."

Katherine responded to his commands and started teasing him with her dancing around the room. Jonathan enjoyed watching her getting undressed. The sheer sight of her nakedness excited him. He was watching her undress until she had nothing on except the gift he gave her.

With piqued curiosity, she slid under the cover with special ease. His groping at her left every inch of her body numb. But this time he took extra time and consideration to make sure that she was enjoying the playful enjoyment of their lovemaking. His lips moved down her thigh, nearing what was already waiting for him. She was moving with slow, pulsating rhythm, and they both relished in the delights that were about to take place.

Katherine was feeling the mounds of flesh skimming over her body, exciting her with new feelings of satisfaction. His male hardness was throbbing with excitement and entering her sweet softness brought both of them to a new understanding and appreciation for each other.

The cool air blowing throw the open windows reminded Katherine of the first time she ever made love. As a young girl growing up in the Midwest, life was so simple. People were honest and more trusting. A handshake was a person's honor. She wanted to bestow that honesty, but things didn't quite work out for her. All she ever wanted was a husband whom she adored and children to fill her life with joy. She didn't want to fall in love with a married man, but Jonathan was a total shock.

Jonathan was very rambunctious, and his strength was quiet obvious. He gathered himself up and his loved one with the utmost of power, yet gentleness from the bed. With the greatest of ease, he placed Katherine and himself in the tub of luscious, warm water. Without moving, Katherine laid her head back on Jonathan's chest. She closed her eyes and allowed herself to drift into a state of nothingness. Her body was floating and feeling weightlessness. She never wanted to return to reality. Yet, she knew that reality was slowly easing its way back into their lives and it was time for both to part.

Jonathan decided to stay and shower, but Katherine had to start home. Before leaving, Jonathan told her that it was important that they not see each other for a while outside of the office.

"Samantha is really suspicious. It would be better if we waited a few weeks to meet like this again."

"It's going to be very difficult to keep my hands off of you." Katherine explained, "I want to hold you. I want to be with you. If we were to go somewhere else, maybe then, we could meet more often. I can't get enough of you. I think about you constantly, my darling Jonathan."

Jonathan and Samantha were husband and wife only in name. Too many years went by without talking about their problems, mostly stemming from overbearing family interference. As strong as Jonathan was, he was no match for Beatrice and Marcus Rudolph, his in-laws. He just tired of answering to Samantha's family.

He wanted to be his own boss.

As Katherine dressed, Jonathan dried himself and climbed back into bed. He was quite satisfied with himself after his remarks and continued to drift downward in the bed as well as into sleep. Katherine kissed him on the forehead and tickled his ear with sweet whispers. She then tiptoed out the door. Before leaving, Katherine reached into her purse and slid his present next to his body.

"Jonathan, you are my life. I will always love you forever." She sighed.

The box contained antique cufflinks she bought a few months ago from a jewelry dealer who bought only estate jewelry. Jonathan loved them, but he really didn't want her to spend her money. With the last remaining kisses tingling her lips, she forced herself to leave, for she wasn't looking forward to the ride back home. She was exhausted. As she was about to open the door, allowing the night air in, she could hear him saying as she closed the door behind her, "Katherine, I'm the luckiest man."

Katherine glanced around the darkened area with restrictive movements. With Samantha being so suspicious, she didn't want to be noticed. "You fool, Katherine," she said to herself. "Nobody's out here in the middle of the woods watching." From what Jonathan told her, Samantha really was suspicious of his movements.

# Chapter 2

The next day, Katherine decided to dress in her usual linen-type suit, finishing it off with her new present. She decided to wear her favorite red V-neck sweater her mother made one Christmas. It was cable stitched with small detailed appliqués of gold flowers. Whenever she wore gifts her mother made for her, she always felt closer to her. After losing her mother to cancer nine years earlier, her personal items and gifts became more precious than ever.

The quaint garden-like apartment with its colonial shutter seemed to allow too much daylight in because it didn't filter out the rays of the morning sun which always woke her too early, even before the alarm clock. Friends suggested buying drapes for her bedroom, but drapes reminded her of hotel rooms, and this was her home. The white lace overlay above on the valances and matching lampshades made an almost dreamlike fairy-tale existence. Wedgewood blue was the accent color placed strategically around the rooms for total relaxation, giving a feeling of country French.

She loved her folk art and homemade items which was quite apparent by glancing around her home. She was able to put a small deposit down on this North Shore, Cape Cod, style apartment. It was actually called a one-story New England duplex. Being so close to New Hampshire, she was able to travel up through the hills of three bordering states in her leisure, exploring old farms for some discarded relics. The best company was your own and for many days on end, she did just that.

She loved old picture frames with old pictures of people in them. She was always asking the seller questions about their history. She didn't need to know them. She just wanted to know that they were real people with families or maybe a history behind the faces and frames.

Katherine was the type of person who thought that if you had cultural things around the house, then you could become cultured. She didn't have an opportunity to be as educated as her friends at work. Katherine only graduated high school because of finances. College was out of the question at the time.

She didn't have any real images of her father since her mother told her that he died. Never any pictures. She thought that was very strange but knew not to ask any more questions since it always seems to upset her mother. Her grandmother ended up living with them. Katherine didn't ask any questions about him because it always irritated her mother when she did. As a very young girl, Katherine learned to be very sensitive toward her mother. It seemed that she was always in a state of depression. Katherine didn't know this at her age, but she knew that something wasn't right.

When her mother lost her job at the factory, the three of them had to move into a smaller apartment. Mary worked two jobs. As an Irish immigrant, Mary was only able to get housekeeping jobs for the wealthy American families.

The summers in Iowa were dreadfully hot and sticky, while cold winter days made Katherine run into Grandma Nettie's warm waiting arms. She always had extra hugs for Katherine and told wonderful stories, which fascinated her for hours. She always told her of the days in Ireland and then coming to America. She spoke of the rough seas, the people herded together at the bottom of the vessel, and how often they prayed that the ship would sink.

Katherine's heart was slowly being broken. Katherine didn't want to believe that her grandma was as sick as she pretended that she wasn't. Grandma Nettie gave her a very special family Bible with fragmented pages and moldy scents. She told her that this book would play an important role in her life. Grandma told her that fate would play a drastic part in her future, but she must find her own destiny. Katherine didn't understand the rambling words from her grandmother just before she died. So she packed up the books and the Bible with other old papers. Katherine's grandmother died on November twenty-fourth, and Katherine always lit a candle at St. Christopher's. She never gave much thought to the message. Katherine learned at an early age to survive with what she had. After she graduated from high school, she set out to find her destiny. She always wanted to see the ocean and decided to go to the Boston area. She then settled outside of Boston since that was the first entry her mother had when she came to America.

Katherine worked into her job by listening to others and staying at work long after others went home. Persistence, tenacity, and perseverance persuaded the bosses of the mill to give her a chance to move into a respected position. Katherine was always watching and learning but always inspire those around her to better educate themselves. She always wanted to be at the top. She had to prove to herself that she could do it.

She loved having beautiful things around her. She bought her china and glassware piece by piece until she had a whole set. Silver was something that she had already decided was going to have to wait. Frills and lace were in her life. Her house lavished in it, and she moderately brought it into the office without doing too much. It was still a man's world. Bringing too much femininity into the workplace was still something the business world would have to set aside.

Katherine started noticing that her clothes were somewhat roomier than usual. She was back to losing too much weight. She reached a size that she tried to maintain and felt that she was most attractive. Her only problem was, was that Katherine didn't know how attractive she really was to others and herself.

There were always the stares from men. Whenever she entered a room, women would scrutinize her to the finishing touches. Men would glance, quickly looking at her hips, and then their eyes went to what seemed perfectly shaped breasts. Men were always on guard.

They felt that their awareness of her presence would give them away. They didn't want them to be noticed by whomever they were with, usually their wives. Without acknowledging their sudden desires, they would turn away with a sheepish, almost boyish expression on their faces. Then, they prayed that no one else recognized their symptoms.

Men were not intimidated by Katherine's beauty, but many were longing to be touched by those hands. Men noticed her long graceful fingers as part of her body poetry. And she did have poetry surrounding her. She had the habit of orchestrating her conversations by allowing her hands to flow in such directions that men would actually feel the rhythm that stimulated their attraction. They were like radar sensors emitting currents that were felt only by them.

# Chapter 3

O n December first, two years ago, Katherine's life was altered into a state of total confusion by the entrance of Jonathan Arpel. Standing at the door of the conference room, Jonathan was in the threshold. The closeness when passing, annoyed her for a second, and for what reason, she really didn't know. She thought most men would have stepped aside when a lady entered a room. He just stood in the way. Maybe it was the gentlemen's intense stare or smug smile that sent a chill about her. She had seen them before but usually brushed them off.

"Ladies and gentlemen, I would like to introduce our new president and owner, Mr. Jonathan Arpel. He has purchased our company with the hopes of taking it to new heights, Worldwide Fabrications, Inc. Mr. Douglas Scottingham was finished with his introduction.

If only the walls could murmur the whispers those wonderful tales of old into listening ears of today's youth.

Katherine was grossly involved with what Mr. Scottingham, chairman of the board, was trying to say, when Jonathan stood up and asked Katherine how she felt about the takeover and what her thoughts were on increasing employee participation. She was thrown directly into the limelight, which was something she wasn't prepared for, and yet, eyeballed Mr. Jonathan Arpel, new owner, back and said all she had to say. There were some faces being made by two of the board members but were quieted with a silent gesture by Mr. Jonathan Arpel.

Katherine had been in the mill for the last seven years. She grew to love the people that made Worldwide Fabrications what it is today, but she also had heard, it was their poor investments that made the old owners sell.

This introduction was the first time she met him personally since he bought the company. There had been rumors. No one had laid eyes on him. No one really knew who he was. He kept his identity quiet so he could move around the mill, getting ideas from unsuspecting people—the workers, a stranger moving laundry buckets around with fabric strips from the cutting rooms to the dumpsters.

With some satisfaction in presentation, Katherine stopped talking. Jonathan had the secretary read back some figures and introductions of ideas that seemed to make sense. Mr. Arpel nodded his head and left the room.

Upon his exit, there seemed to be a complete atmospheric change. Katherine was once again able to breathe. She didn't realize that the pounding in her head was the drumming of her heart. It seemed to be a deafening sound, and whatever was said after he left, she couldn't recognize it as language. The shocking murmuring and the confusion had left her in dire need for the ladies' room. It left her trembling her way through the corridors into the powder room, where she tried to collect herself.

She had this incredible desire to put Mr. Arpel in his place, but her mere thinking of him and his undivided attention upon her face was exciting, and yet, actually infuriated her. She couldn't decide if it was his very expensive silk suit, the way his pants tugged around his male parts, or the stupid little vein on the left side of his neck that popped out around his collared shirts that antagonized her. His entire presence, both physically and psychologically, caught Katherine off guard. His complete posture captured her imagination. He was amazingly handsome. His jet-black hair caressed the nape of his neck, touching those very starched collared shirts that she watched her mother iron for the wealthy.

Mr. Arpel was at least six feet tall, with broad shoulders, but it was his controlling attitude that peaked her dislike for him. She had this very burning desire to be very close to him, and the smell of his cologne lingered not just in her nostrils but in her brain. If she closed her eyes, she felt that he was still next to her, and she could feel him closing in on her fantasies.

This had never happened to her with anyone before. He had affected her in such a way that it was quite earth-shattering. She wasn't used to being altered into her state of confusion. She was mad at Mr. Jonathan Arpel for putting her on the spot. She did find it quite exhilarating to be listened to by a board of nine men, four of whom were new and the others were people she had worked with for years. People always found it hard to change the manner of doing business. Things here were about to change.

# Chapter 4

When Katherine arrived at the office the next day, after a totally sleepless night, there was a humming from friends. Something big was going to happen. Katherine was unaware that it was going to affect her.

Katherine was trying to make it through the average morning of going through her mail and finalizing reports with her staff. Mathew, who worked right under her in her department, was of the greatest help. He was a younger man making Katherine's life a lot easier. This morning there were too many interruptions to get anything done.

"Good morning, Katherine. Do you have any idea what's going on in this office? There are rumblings from upstairs."

Mathew just came running into her office mumbling something about a traffic problem. She just shrugged her shoulders trying not to get tied up in this conversation. There were speculations. She told a couple of secretaries to get off the phones and get to work. She had to proceed with business at hand. Katherine told her girlfriend Mattie that she would meet her for lunch at the restaurant around the corner for a quick lunch, except it never happened that way. It was at that time, chaos from the outer office.

Mr. Jonathan Arpel stood in front of Katherine's desk. Without a word, he pointed to follow him through the corridors to the elevators. There was total silence in the offices, and yet, a hush traveled through each person's glance to witness this parade of people.

Katherine was feeling very shaky and nervous. The palms of her hands were all clammy. Again, the pounding in her ears made it difficult to hear conversation, but of course, there wasn't any. She could feel the beads of sweat trickle down the back of her neck. She was standing in the elevator with Mr. Arpel. He was to her left, and Mr. Standers, VP of operations, to her right.

Both of the women in the elevator with them seemed to be ready to write whatever was said from either men. No further instructions or conversation followed. Katherine was just lacking sensation in her body. "Please don't faint," she told herself.

When they reached the eighth floor, doors opened. To Katherine's surprise, she was facing a crowd of people who were clapping their hands and congratulating her for a job well done. She thanked everyone but didn't know what they were talking about. Mr. Arpel was about to make things clear to her and introduce Katherine to a few unfamiliar faces. Ms. Katherine Donahue was about to be promoted to vice president of human resources along with a very hefty salary increase. All made possible by Mr. Arpel.

Mr. Jonathan Arpel began to speak. "Katherine Donahue has earned the notoriety of being a woman with a good head on her shoulders. She also has a longtime understanding of the heartbeat of this company. I purchased this factory for a long-term growth potential. I didn't know that people like Katherine came along with my purchase. I am very proud to have someone like her with us and am sure that we will be increasing the company's equity along with a number of employees to fill our growth. Katherine, with a deep appreciation for your dedication and hard work, I want to introduce you to your new office. Remodel it in any way you wish, and it's just the beginning."

Mr. Arpel stopped talking and opened the door for Katherine's inspection.

By now she was almost in tears and had to bite her inner cheeks so hard that she thought that blood would come gushing out of her mouth. She formally accepted the promotion by a simple trembling handshake.

"Thank you for putting your trust in me. I will do everything not to let you down." Katherine realized that she was looking into a sea of the bluest eyes she had ever seen. She was completely caught off guard by this man! Katherine was in shock.

Within minutes, everyone, including Mr. Arpel left, and Katherine was standing inside her new office with a young woman who introduced herself as Elizabeth.

"I prefer to be called Liz, if you don't mind. I am your new secretary. If you need anything at all, please don't hesitate to ask me. I'm still attending the local college at night taking some marketing courses." Katherine liked her immediately. "I want to increase my knowledge of the advertising media." Liz explained that her real goal was to break into major TV and radio programming. She wanted to be a part of it. Katherine admired her honesty.

Liz was maybe around twenty-one years of age. She had a very upbeat attitude. Katherine couldn't help but like her and knew that they would get along.

Katherine was about to get her head together when there was a knock at the door and a few of her friends from the fifth floor came in with a catered lunch from the local deli. She was so shocked over what had happened that tears of joy and excitement, yet confusion, filled her with a wonderful feeling of accomplishment.

She hugged everybody. "Thank you all. I was as much surprised as you. Thank you again for helping me, especially you, Mathew."

Katherine had a flashback and closed her eyes. She remembered when she started out for her first interview, fresh out of high school, and she had such fears that she wouldn't have the right qualifications. She was applying for a job as a file clerk, but they needed someone with a little knowledge of computers. She filled the void. She hoped that she would never have to go through another interview in her life.

"Excuse me, I have to go to the little girls' room."

Katherine then left her friends in her new office and had to head for the ladies room. Whatever makeup she started out with today was totally smudged off. She noticed the soft carpet under her feet cushioning her so she wouldn't fall off, and yet fall off what?

She couldn't believe that her life was beginning to take on a different shape, a different form. Oh, where is the bathroom?

Gazing into the mirror making sure that this was not a dream, she pinched herself. She saw a woman with her messy face smeared with tears and makeup, but a woman who knew that her world would never be the same.

In total silence, she closed her eyes, placed her hands on each side of the sink, and found her voice speaking out loud.

"Thank you, Lord, for all you have given me."

With that, Katherine left the ladies' room.

# Chapter 5

Samantha was getting out of her silver-blue Mercedes with the components for making a fine dinner. The Websters were coming over for dinner. Shirley, the cook and housekeeper, was taking her day off. Samantha didn't mind. Her first love was cooking, and it gave her an opportunity to be creative with international cuisines. She wanted to experiment on some dishes from their last trip to Europe.

As she was fumbling for the keys to the house, the phone was ringing. The bundles of groceries were on the way down to knee-level. She decided to grab the bags, find the keys, and let the phone ring. She always hated not answering the phone. Not knowing who was on the other end of the telephone was always torture. The phone would just have to wait.

The french doors Jonathan decided to put in, gave the back of the house a very dramatic look. They were beautiful but weren't very functional when trying to get in from the side. Samantha was really tired from all her shopping and her workout at the club. All she wanted to do was start dinner and then shower leisurely. As she removed her clothes, she could see that she wasn't as thin as when she met Jonathan. She was always aware of her weight problem, and working out helped keep things in the right places, but lately it was harder. She started thinking back when they married and couldn't believe that it was almost nine years ago this coming May.

They were so taken with each other. For the first time in Samantha's life, she was on her own. She was going to make her own decisions. They dated for a short time, and then they decided to elope. Wow, what a shock! She knew that her mother would feel robbed of the joy of seeing her only daughter get married. At times she could feel the tremendous resentment from her. Now, Mother Beatrice, as she preferred to be called, was no one to reckon with. She was a very powerful and overbearing woman. Her father, Mr. Marcus Rudolph, was, in a way, relieved that she took a stand against Beatrice. Samantha didn't even allow herself to consider that it might be Daddy's money that attracted Jonathan to her. Her family members were of old aristocratic stock in Germany and Austria.

As Samantha was finishing up dressing, she was asking herself what happened over the years. They had such dreams, such hopes and aspirations. Jonathan had everything he needed except the intimate satisfaction from his wife. What did she ever do wrong? They never should have stayed in the big house with her parents so long.

Their small bickering started right after about a year of marriage and Jonathan wanted to leave the house then, Samantha recalled. Beatrice insisted that they stay and try to work things out. Jonathan couldn't understand how Samantha changed her mind, and living under mother's roof was not an option but an obligation.

Samantha just couldn't see it. There were never any real arguments, just indifference. She now questioned herself every day and realized that he was right. They grew apart in those first few years. Now she seemed to want to rekindle what they had. Deep down in her heart, she still loved him very much.

When she put makeup on, Samantha was considered good-looking. Samantha knew what she had to do in order to be attractive. She had to work at it. Her blond hair was too curly, and she was always having to straighten it. She held it back with barrettes and pins but insisted on wearing strange little hats to cover it all up. She was thrilled that bell-bottoms pants were in. This way she could cover up her ankles, and of course, platform shoes made her look much taller than she really was. She always thought that she could sense things about people. She watched friends' reactions meeting Jonathan. He was absolutely handsome. There was an obvious tilt of their head or a raised eyebrow and then a quick look at Samantha and then another glance at Jonathan. Samantha couldn't quite understand why such a handsome man like Jonathan had married her. He was always going out with so many radiant beauties at school.

Jonathan came from an average-income family who pushed him through school. He was in graduate school, and Samantha was working on her teacher's degree. After Jonathan's graduation exercises, his parents were in a fatal car crash while returning home. He never really got to say goodbye to his parents. He regretted them driving and not flying like he wanted them to do. Getting married seemed to be the best thing for both of them. They married, and Samantha dropped out of school. She always wanted to return to her studies but lost interest. After all, she was a married lady now and had her husband.

There was insurance money, which he used to start his mortgage company. Jonathan absolutely refused to use any of Samantha's money and had to live on what he earned. Even though he was very determined to be on his own, he gave in to the family request to live with them. A mistake that cost him his marriage.

After all, Samantha was the third-generation money, and she never found having it a problem. She thought everybody had it. She was schooled in the finest Swiss boarding schools and sent to college of her choice with a very large endowment to the school. There had never been any obstacles in her life other than her mother's love. Samantha always felt that her mother was mad at her. She didn't know why, nor was there something she had done to upset her. She had heard through family discussion that her mother's marriage to her father, Marcus Rudolph, was prearranged by her grandfather, Sir Henry Von Burger.

Samantha always fit into everybody's lifestyle. Her best memories were in the grand old kitchen with the servants preparing meals. She loved helping at dinner parties. If Mother Beatrice found out, it would be looks casted down in outrage. The mere thought of Samantha in the kitchen with the servants was unthinkable. What if her friends could see! It was unbefitting for the granddaughter of Sir Henry Von Burger to be found in the kitchen.

There were always wonderful smells coming from it. Samantha remembered the breads, cookies, and French pastries lined up on racks, cooling off on the opened windowsills. In the dead of winter, the baking of biscuits and breads permeated through the house, keeping out the bleak, stormy air. No matter how bad it was out there, Samantha always felt that she was in some protected custody by its warmth.

Samantha always wanted to help make the beds and fold linens. She was scolded by mother again and again. Samantha was sent to boarding school. She always felt that her mother wanted to get her out of the house. She was not even able to pick up a needle and thread to sew a button or fix her playthings in her room. They were done by the servants. She had a life made in heaven, except if you don't know that you're there, then what good is it?

# Chapter 6

Samantha had placed the Rosenthal and Grand Barque dinnerware carefully around the dining room table with the proper candlesticks. She received them from Great-Grandma for their wedding. The linen was of the finest money could buy from a French silk house in Paris that no longer existed. Grandfather bought the shop just to keep the flow of silks coming into the States.

Their dining room almost had the look of a library since the walls were lined with books. Many of them were in Samantha's family for years and were first editions. Rare books of all kinds were placed under glass locked in one corner. To give the room gentleness, Samantha placed fresh flowers in the center of the table and on the sideboards. Samantha was very pleased with herself.

"Never use fake flowers, Samantha. It's a sign of bad breeding," Mother's voice echoed out in her head.

Samantha was actually getting the whole dinner together when the phone rang again.

"Hello, Sam, it's me. I'm going to have to be home very late or not at all," Jonathan went on. "I have a merger I'm working on, and my work must be completed by tomorrow. The necessary papers just came over by personal courier from Japan. I must put my figures with theirs. If this deal is going to go through before the end of the new year, I have to do this now."

Samantha's heart fell to the floor and rebuffed, "Jonathan, you did know that the Websters were coming over tonight for dinner? They were going to give us our early Christmas gift since they will be in Florence for the holidays." Samantha was trying to be very sweet over the phone showing her disappointment. She was really fuming. "They should be here in about an hour, and dinner is almost completed. Isn't there any way possible that you could sneak home just for dinner and then go back to the office?"

Samantha was hearing this from Jonathan over and over again for the last year. He seemed to find different excuses not to come home on time for dinner. When they were married for two years living at Beatrice's, Jonathan always was able to make their nightly dinners on time. It all started in their own home when business was starting to broaden from the States to Europe.

Dining together was the true sign of reputable families. It was part of Samantha's upbringing. "You always serve dinner at the same time every day. It gives you a proper point of focus," quoted Beatrice. You would think that Samantha would get used to it. Jonathan had an undertone in his voice, and Samantha didn't like what she was thinking. He made his best effort to apologize to her, but it wasn't enough. Samantha knew that some of his business was pleasure and she had to do something about it. She would have to look into this matter. With that, he heard the smash of the receiver hit the base of the phone.

In her own mind, she so wanted to believe him, and Samantha should have realized that most people of average means had to work. They had to put in extra hours to achieve, but with her upbringing, Daddy was always home. She thought her husband should be home too.

Jonathan was making a name for himself in the industry, and he didn't want it to appear to people that he couldn't find his own money. He scheduled his acquisitions and gathered his capital from different sources, enabling him to make the deals he wanted.

Samantha was already on the phone after she fumbled with her address book. She was calling someone she didn't want to know. She was given their name from her accountant. He had been used by him in other cases. The phone was ringing, and an answering service picked up.

"This is the office of Reliable Investigations. Please leave a message. We will get back to you as soon as possible. Please wait for the beep."

Samantha was so frustrated. All she could do was, again, smash the phone down on the base. She would call another time. She would have to catch her husband in the arms of business some other time. Dinner had to be prepared.

The Websters were coming over for dinner, and Mother always said the show must go on. She was always remembering the small instructions pounded into a child of good taste, good breeding, good character, and substance.

"'That is what makes the difference between them and us. The rich and the poor, my darling." Samantha always thought her mother was such a snob, but then again, she began to believe the old monologues of childhood.

"Good stock, that's what counts," Beatrice insisted.

# Chapter 7

T wo weeks to Christmas, which was always very hectic for Jonathan, but he was forced to stay on track. He had his staff preparing the office for the holidays and buying gifts for everybody. He was in a fabulous mood lately, and his whole staff could see it. Even Samantha noticed a difference. "It's just that the holidays are coming up and I am having a very profitable year," Jonathan claimed.

There he was, just four floors above hers, and his mind was already on the down elevator. Jonathan was at the helm of his business for the last fourteen months. He could see many things going on that he liked and yet, didn't expect it to happen so soon.

Many of the employees came to him and expressed their thankfulness for his purchase and his plans for the company. After all, it was their jobs at stake, and they wanted to keep them. But that was just the small of it. Katherine was doing such a creative job with employee relationships that there was a real difference, and people were showing it.

He had seen her many times walking through the building, and she inadvertently walked a little faster. She had many board meetings, but Mr. Arpel was always out of town or listening on an intercom. She was always in a hurry and didn't know how to handle herself. She was so unsure of herself, even now, around him. She had been seen in the employee's cafeteria by Jonathan's personal assistant that morning. He gave Katherine the message. Figures for the insurance company had to be brought to Mr. Arpel's office around five that evening.

His excitement showed, and leaving nothing to chance, Jonathan had Jacob personally deliver the message. Jacob was a complete miracle for Jonathan. Jacob had seen her many times before at meetings and coffee clutches but never made the connection until now. Even though he wasn't interested in women, he did understand. Jacob had made the arrangements for that evening, and Katherine was supposed to leave all the paperwork with him. When she arrived upstairs, Katherine looked for Jacob. He was not in his office. Instead, Jonathan popped his head out from behind the desk.

"Excuse me, but I'm just looking for something." Katherine stood frozen to the carpet.

"What in the world are you doing, and can I help you?" Jonathan couldn't even answer.

Katherine started to melt. Katherine realized that they were alone without anyone there. She went completely numb and said something about some papers Jacob told her to bring up. Jonathan directed her into a chair and with a soothed look of a small child who just got his way. She didn't care.

Their closeness was apparent immediately, and they backed off. Jonathan stood next to her.

"Thank you for bringing these to my office." Before he could stop himself, he was trying to explain that he needed her help and asked if they could have dinner tonight. There was such an urgency that they both knew what was in store for that evening. Katherine could feel her skin turning red, and with the smallest of a voice, she replied in the affirmative.

She had to be near him. She had to be with him. She wanted to be in this man's arms so badly. All she knew was that this man called Jonathan Arpel was something out of her dreams, and she had to make it a reality.

They stood close in the private elevator without saying one word to each other. Only glances were allowed and a small jester of the head to one side indicating Jonathan's deep desire that he wanted her. It was a sacred moment for both of them. Not a word was spoken. Katherine felt her face flush and hoped that he didn't notice. Their eyes were glued to each other's. Jonathan was making love to her without one touch. Not a word was spoken. She could feel the flow of energy given off, and her mind was making up all kinds of images. The tingling at the ends of her fingertips rested on her own lips. She then gently kissed them not realizing till afterward that they were her own.

Jonathan was staring at the most beautiful creation that God put on this earth. He was about to have her, every inch of her. Standing next to her with eyes peeled together, he could taste her, smell her, and yet, not touch her, at least not yet, not here. His muscles in his groins were aching, and his heart was beating so fast that he felt like a schoolkid with his first puppy love. But this was not puppy love. Jonathan, for the first time in his life, was capturing everything he had ever wanted, read about, and dreamed about in this woman called Katherine Donahue. He closed his eyes only for a moment to remember.

Jacob had made reservations at an inn using his own name, Jacob Arnold. The cottage was being arranged and dinner prepared by the owners. Since this was a bed-and-breakfast arrangement, Jacob had to offer quite a sum for their talents. Everything was cooked and delivered to cottage #3 ahead of time. A splendid evening was about to take place.

Katherine rode in the car seated as closely as possible to the door. She was clinging onto the handle as Jonathan drove. If Katherine let go, she might attack him, and that wouldn't prove too healthy. She was studying his profile as he drove in the dark and wondered if she was only seeing something in him that wasn't really there. She saw such strength and sensitivity, and yet a deep need for loving. She had to have him. Not a word was spoken.

Jonathan drove with the greatest of care knowing that he had the most precious cargo onboard. He couldn't believe that she was here. Thinking back to when he first saw her seemed so long ago. It has taken him so long to get to this decision. He had had so many sleepless nights just thinking of her. He was left exhausted for work.

Samantha noticed and wanted to call the family doctor for some advice. There had been little or no sex between them for some time, and this restlessness Jonathan was experiencing affected everything. When he did make love to Samantha, she told him that she thought that she was making love to a total stranger. His mind was somewhere else, yet his actions seemed motivated by hunger. Wives know the workings of their husbands. When something changes, there is a reason.

Katherine's breath was taken away when she entered this little cottage holding on to Jonathan. The smell of pine and woods were everywhere. A fire was roaring in the floor-to-ceiling fireplace. When Katherine saw to what length Jonathan had gone through to impress her, she started to tremble. Her face was radiant and glowed from the fire's reflections on her. There was no more waiting.

With shaking hands, Jonathan started to unbutton Katherine's blouse. She could feel the tension, making Jonathan shake with anticipation. She held on to his hands and guided him to the fur rug that was stretched out in front of the roaring fire. They both knelt down in front of each other while the flames played dancing images on their bodies. The magic from the fire, the smells of the cottage, and the desire between two people could be easily felt between them. The hair lengths from the fur rug seemed to grab hold around Katherine's body, and she started floating on this magical carpet. Jonathan started again with the buttons, and they seemed to part without any problems. Katherine was opening Jonathan's shirt and pulling it out from his belted pants when a large crackle from the fire snapped them into a sexual frenzy.

Jonathan was shedding his clothes, and Katherine was undressing herself. The urgency to be as one was driving them into a ravenous sensation that not even a hurricane could stop. He was engineering himself to taste every curve of her magnificent body and drink her exotic wines that were yet to come. Her body against his was no match for any man. He was totally out of control and wanted to devour her, except she had more control now. Katherine then took the lead in their lovemaking. She placed her hands over his and placed his fingers deep inside her swelling crevice. Katherine began feathering kisses and light whimsical jesters to Jonathan's body, leaving him moaning for more. Their bodies were entwined with such tender stroking and beads of sweat clinging from each other. When Jonathan began to mount her like a champion stallion, Katherine started to moan. His firm pulsating organ was exploding with desire. She began challenging his rhythm. Together their bodies were distorted with raw, passionate love exploding with every thrust. Katherine had never been made love to with such force of strength, and her limbs were moving aimlessly. Her mind reflecting back when she first saw the ocean. Watching the pounding of crashing waves smash down against mounds of rocks, causing a collision of energy. The witnessing of such a force was being felt at this very moment. Katherine was in a world of total pleasure, and she never wanted it to end. Jonathan had proven to be quite a lover.

There had been quite a lot of drifting or dreaming in and out of sleep. Their bodies didn't move, yet Katherine thought she was lifted up and moved. Jonathan's arms were wrapped around her chest and waist with her head nestled in his neck, breathing down his ear and nibbling on the lobe. With the slowest and deepest voice, he could muster up, "Katherine, I love you." Tears were running down her cheeks.

"And I love you, Jonathan," whispered Katherine.

They were both lost in the taste and smells of each other. After an hour or so, Katherine lifted her head and suggested they get something to eat. Jonathan was clinging to her in fear that she might get up and be gone out of his life. He wanted to slow it down. He didn't want to move. He started kissing her all over, making small circular movements with his tongue under her ear. This was sending thrilling sensual feelings throughout her body. Her instincts were aroused again. She knew then that they were going to have to wait for dinner just a little longer. All she knew was that she had to have him. They fell into another sexual frenzy. Both were trying to capture the essence of each other.

Jacob had asked the owners of the bed-and-breakfast to prepare something easy to warm up and place the wine on ice, which they did. When one entered the cottage, you could smell the pinewood walls and wooly fabrics from the bed coverings. Old lanterns were hung from the ceilings in every room and placed on the mantelpiece over the fireplace. Overstuffed furniture with red/blue plaid with fringe draped over two matching chairs and one much worn sofa. The table, in knotty pine wood, was set with plenty of candles and a fresh basket of bread. With the slowest of motion, they grinned at each other and started to ascend on this lovely meal for a different kind of nourishment. They finally feasted on a meal that they only devoured for the sake of eating. They were in the best of company. There they sat across from each other actually licking their fingers and sipping on wine innocent of the fact that there they sat, completely powerless in their nakedness.

"Katherine, I adore you. I have been dreaming of you ever since I first saw you at the mill. I am absolutely crazy about you," Jonathan whispered over the wine glass. He played with the stem, demonstrating how fragile this moment was. Yes, fragile and delicate. Jonathan didn't want to ruin this time of truth. After all, he was a married man. He was taking quite a chance. If this doesn't turn out to go his way, he must somehow clarify this and go on. There was a lot at risk.

Katherine fingered her hair that was feathered down across her shoulders back so he could see her magnificent face. Her eyes were pleading with him for she was studying his face under a new light. This time she realized that they had taken a great chance by coming here and turning their lives into an affair. This was not supposed to happen.

"Jonathan, I knew full well why you wanted me and for how long. There was always something going on between us. I tried not to show it. I guess I didn't do too good. I was falling in love with you, Jonathan Arpel, a married man, the moment I first saw you. I'm not sorry that this happened. I hope that whatever happens in the future is for us to create. I am truly in love with you."

Katherine had placed her wineglass to the right side of her and was reaching out to him. By this time, Jonathan was sitting right next to her. "How could I be so blessed?" Jonathan whispered.

Jonathan and Katherine rested their bodies on the magic carpet, and they drifted off to even new pleasures. She practically manhandled him into a sexual state that he never knew. Katherine devoured him and drank his love potion. Katherine, with her magnificent mind, body, and spirit, made Jonathan feel things never felt before with anybody. She was using her witchcraft, and Jonathan was certainly under her spell.

# Chapter 8

The hours passed, and Jonathan knew that they had a drive back home. Katherine dressed herself, brushed her hair, and was pinning it back with combs when she laughed at Jonathan fiddling with his shirt and then helped him to find his shoes and socks. Why do men always misplace them? She had to keep him off her or they never would have gotten out of there. He couldn't keep to himself.

Jonathan finished getting dressed and then opened the door to go out. The blast of cold air caught them off guard. They were shocked back into reality. They knew that life would be different for the both of them.

Katherine was totally unprepared for that night. The night that was about to change her whole life. Love had entered her life, and she was going to hold on to it as long as possible.

Jonathan had her snuggle up to him in the car, and together they traveled back to the office, where Katherine would pick up her car. They both were in their own worlds of contentment, and they enjoyed their silence together. They truly appreciated their personal privilege of being as one. They were going to weave their fibers of their own love into the most glorious fabric ever created by man.

# Chapter 9

S amantha was sleeping in the large bed when Jonathan came tiptoeing into the dressing area.

"Jonathan, is that you?"

Jonathan was very tired from the ride back from the cottage, and he was quite curt with Samantha. "I'm your husband. Who do you think it is, your lover?

Samantha didn't look up from the pillow to see what time it was. She knew that it was extremely late.

"Come to bed and let me make you feel comfortable after your hard day and night at work." Samantha's sarcasm resonated across the bedroom.

"Samantha, I'm exhausted, and my meetings didn't work out the way I wanted. Our figures that I needed didn't match. I'm not going to be able to buy what I need to enable proper profits for next year." Jonathan really did come across very honest. Samantha was beginning to believe him. She always wanted to believe him. With that, she went to sleep, and he took a sigh of relief.

During breakfast, Samantha and Jonathan sat in the dining room not saying too much to each other. Samantha couldn't wait for him to leave. She was going to make that call again. Instead, Samantha decided to pay a visit to her mother right after breakfast. That was strange to begin with, since she knew that her parents were very late sleepers. She didn't want to miss her. Her mother would have to understand. She decided to admit to her mother that maybe her marriage was in trouble.

The house was massive. The tall elm and oak trees hovering over the long driveway insisted that one was about to enter a world only known to the very rich. Each tree perfectly shaped, and the lawn, manicured, gave the house a dimension relative to those who lived there. This grand English tudor was in the family from Samantha's grandfather. He came to America to find his fortune in the land. He started a small wicker furniture factory and then branched out to fabrics and textiles.

Grandfather Von Burger was a calculating individual with his hands into everything. Nothing ever passed his mind or escaped his knowledge of the business at hand. Leather for heels and soles on army boots. He even furnished material to the government for uniforms.

Rumors had it that he was involved with the wrong kind of people at one time. Government agencies were looking into him. They would only warn him of the investigations since he was such an important person to the development of this country. When prohibition was voted in, Grandfather was there. It was rumored that he was a bootlegger bringing liquor in from Canada. Nothing escaped his visions.

Samantha was on her second cup of coffee when her mother entered the dining room, shocked to see her daughter.

"Darling, what are you doing here so early?" gasped Beatrice.

"I just decided to visit and have a chat with you, Mother. Is Father up yet?" Samantha noticed something strange about mother this morning. She just didn't look quite right.

By now, Beatrice sat at the end of the table almost tripping over her long day gown with the tassels flowing to the floor. They waited for the servants to leave the area so conversation couldn't be overheard.

"What is wrong, Mother? You look troubled."

"Oh, it's nothing."

Beatrice was about to digest her grapefruit when Samantha asked, "Mother, have you ever suspected father of cheating on you?"

Beatrice choked and gasped, turning red from lack of oxygen. She couldn't imagine quite a question ever coming from her daughter's lips.

Samantha rambled on trying to explain and apologized at the same time for asking the question. Samantha was quite exhausted from the lack of sleep, and she was questioning her own motives for the questions. She knew that this was very embarrassing. She should have asked the question differently. Like, would a woman know if her husband was having an affair with another woman? What would be the telltale signs? Things like that. Instead, without too much thinking, she blurted out to her mother some ludicrous questions that took her mother by storm.

Beatrice tried to stop choking. "What kind of a question is that?"

"I have to know. It's important to me, and I think Jonathan is having an affair. Do you ever know if your husband is having an affair?" Samantha was now up pacing around the dining room table waiting for an answer.

What was she to do? Her daughter wanted an answer. "Oh my god, is this the moment I've dreaded all these years?" Beatrice knew that this day would come, but where did all the time go? It seemed like a thousand years had gone by. Years of arguing with Marcus. Years of deceit. He always said to leave it alone. The disgrace would rip this family apart. The secret festered itself into every aspect of her marriage. The secret never left them from that moment on. That moment being the day Samantha was born. Every time Beatrice looked at Samantha, it was there.

For some reason, Beatrice felt for the first time she was addressing a question from an old friend that she had been searching for. This time it was her daughter. Maybe, after all these years of being a mother to her, now it was time to be her friend.

She sat there for a few seconds and realized that what she was about to say had never been said to anyone else on this earth. She was about to reveal information that she had withheld from everyone.

She gathered herself firmly on the chair and looked Samantha in the eyes and knew that her daughter would never look at her in the same way ever again.

Beatrice decided to explain that most men, for whatever their needs might be, do have affairs. The time of truth. Her entire body was frozen to the dining chair. What would be Samantha's reaction?

Samantha noticed the difference the moment her mother opened her mouth. There was softness about her expression. A composure that she never saw in her mother. She walked over to her mother and knelt down on the floor, placing her hands on top of her mother's. Samantha could feel the tension in Beatrice's body. Beatrice was mouthing some words, but they weren't coming out.

"Mother, I can't hear you. What is it?" She could feel the nerves in her spine scramble with pain as her mother spoke.

"Samantha, my darling child," Beatrice said in a whisper hardly audible.

Beatrice was overcome with tears running down her weathered face, and at that moment, Samantha was frightened to hear what she was going to say. Samantha was in shock over the change Mother had taken. She was showing emotion, something that Beatrice held back for years. Samantha never saw her shed a tear. Samantha didn't know what her mother was going to divulge.

"Mother, are you all right?"

"No, I'm not."

Beatrice was sobbing with her hands holding up her head off the breakfast table. Her shaking was uncontrollable. Samantha jolted up and pressed against the chair. She stretched her arms around her mother.

Beatrice started over. Her voice was very quiet and calm. She had to tell the secret she and Marcus Rudolph had been keeping for twenty-six years, she waited for this day. This horrible day.

"There are many reasons for men to have affairs with other women. Yes, wives do know when that happens. It's like a seventh sense that God miserably gave us. I think it's best not to know." Beatrice didn't stop talking not even a breath, and went on. "I have something to tell you and have wanted to tell you for many years, but your father convinced me that it was for your sake that we keep this to ourselves."

Samantha was all ears and couldn't believe that her mother was talking to her like this. "What is it that you want to tell me, Mother?"

"Your father had an affair with Mary, our housekeeper, many years ago in this very house. We were married for ten years, and our lovemaking was not of the greatest. Your father was very dissatisfied with me, so he took up with Mary, the housekeeper."

Samantha sat in shock hearing her mother's confession. She was in disbelief. She felt so sorry for her mother. This poor woman had to live with this. Now she was beginning to understand the estrangement between her mother and father all these years. "Go on, Mother."

"Mary was nineteen years old from Ireland with no family here in the United States. She worked for us for years before she got pregnant. At first she told me that it was the neighbor's cook. A few days later, she told me the truth. Marcus Rudolph, my husband, your father, was having his way with our housekeeper in our home. In the home that my father gave us for a wedding present."

Samantha then sat in the chair next to her mother. She was holding on to the arms as if she were on a roller coaster. The pounding in her ears was too much. She had this tremendous desire to scream. She had to hear it all. Samantha's heart was broken for her mother and was sorry for asking the question.

Beatrice continued. She knew now that this should have been said many years ago. Samantha deserved the truth.

"Samantha, your father got Mary in a way that was not proper. She was with a child. I hated your father and was embarrassed for what he did. Your father found a home for Mary to go where a woman of that class went to have babies. Marcus then made arrangements for us to bring the baby into our family as ours. Of course, that's you, my darling Samantha. Mary was placed on a train, and Marcus sent her somewhere to hide our shame."

Beatrice had to pause, take a breath, and then went on. "Please forgive me for not telling you sooner, but I can't stand the look you are giving me right at this moment."

Beatrice was now at Samantha's feet on the floor with uncontrollable crying. Her arms draped over her daughter's thighs. The words had to come out.

"I am not your mother. I was never your mother, and I've hated your father ever since this happened. I have taken my hatred out on you at times," Beatrice finally said it. There was absolute silence in the room.

The temperature in the dining room was unbearable. Sweat was pouring down Samantha's face, and she was paralyzed with this information. "All these years, you kept my real mother's identity from me. This can't be true. I've always felt something not right between us but never thought that anything like this was possible. I always felt like I did something wrong. I now know what I did wrong. I was born. How could you, Mother? I hate you. I hate father even more." Samantha took a breath. "Where is my mother now? What did he do with her? I hate you. I hate him. I hate you all."

Samantha backed off from her mother. Wiping away the tears of horror and shock with the back of her hands, she ran from the house that no longer belonged to her past.

Samantha had to get out.

# *Chapter 10*

Sir Henry Von Burger was having difficulties communicating with the overseas operator. It was extremely common to have cable connection problems, but not for him. He was Sir Henry Von Burger, Samantha's grandfather. He was very annoyed with people who didn't know of him. Henry Von Burger was a demanding individual. He never took no for an answer. He had an unleashing temper that erupted at a moment's notice.

Henry Von Burger was a small-statured man possessing incredible ambition and driven out of self-developed obsession. He was the son of a German immigrant with farming in his blood. He always tinkered with tools, and he was always asking questions about how to make things better or work faster. Living in Iowa gave him the structure needed to take hold of our sacred farmland and make things very basic to man's needs. He created an enormous furniture factory using all the engineering tools modern for those times. He was a forerunner in an endless scope of illusions. People were hired from all around the world and for their technical talents. With Sir Henry Von Burger's know-how, he was able to build a dynasty for those to follow.

Branching out to raw materials into other industries and other countries, his competition started to take notice from around the world. With silks from China and India, wools from Scotland, and even rubber from South America, Henry Von Burger was forced to move to the Boston area. It was easier to receive the large vessels from around the world to Boston ports. Why should he have to ship by rail to Iowa when he could save money and build there? So he moved. The whole family moved.

His movements were like a lion stalking his prey and devouring it whenever desired. Most men, and especially the women, found him to be both fascinating as well as fearful. Sir Henry Von Burger was a man who got what he wanted when he wanted it, and it showed. The womanizing around town was nothing to be made a secret. He had his way with many of the single women and some married. Of course, you didn't mention such things. It was also a sign of wealth at that time to have a mistress or two.

Anyone who had any business dealings with him learned fast how unscrupulous he really was, and revealing such information could cost you your life. There were rumors as to just how he made his fortune. His garish existence repulsed even the most aristocratic Yankee in town.

It was very common to prearrange your daughter's marriage. Beatrice was just a young child when these arrangements were made through connections and business associates. Anyone with breeding always made marriage arrangements for their daughters far in advance of them growing into womanhood. No chances were ever taken, and with the help of a diplomatic family in Switzerland, they were made. Arranged marriages were done only by the wealthiest of families, leaving no chances for mistakes. Families were inspected, with full line of investigations and reputations on the line for the family fortunes. Money had to stay with the money, or should one say, mergers were made at the altar. There was nothing left to chance. A large dowry had been arranged on both sides of the families, and proper documents had to be aligned.

"This is Sir Henry Von Burger calling from the United States, you idiot. Who is this?" shouted the sire. On the other end, you could barely hear the transmission, but only a few words were audible.

"*Summerfest*, two Thursdays from today, 1:00 p.m."

Sir Henry Von Burger hung up the telephone with a sigh and hoped that his daughter, Beatrice, would be at the altar, gloriously happy, with her new husband after the proper introduction within the year. With some relief of conviction, he left the study to gather up the family to tell them of their Thursday-afternoon plans. The ship *Summerfest* would be landing in Boston harbor two weeks' time, Thursday the fourth, at 1:00 p.m., and they were all to be stationed there for a major welcoming committee. The stage was set, and everybody was to follow the set director, which was, of course, Sir Henry Von Burger himself.

# Chapter 11

Marcus Rudolph had gone through days of traveling in order to be properly received by the right people. The arrangements for the intended marriage with Beatrice Von Burger, daughter of Sir Henry Von Burger, an American aristocrat, seemed just to his liking. He didn't have to worry about the money going to some family of lower means. They had more money than he, and Marcus had done business with the family in the past.

All the cartons had to be readied for travel, and the acceptance for the journey came when there was threat of an impending war.

The *Summerfest* was an old, cantankerous vessel having enormous sailings under her sails. The seafaring ship was to set course for "America" with all the earthly possessions belonging to Marcus Rudolph. Glancing over the enormous ship, Marcus could survey his own understanding of his inability to purchase a steamship from the Italians last year. You had to know more than he intended to know, and he let the venture slip through his fingers.

There were arrangements to be made, and Peterson, his valet, handled all the details. Peterson made arrangements of all meals to be delivered to the stateroom. Instructions that no one was to enter Marcus Rudolph's stateroom.

The weather had turned bleak and cold. Everyone was covered up with wool hats, long scarves masking faces, only showing eyes piercing back at you. Long Russian fur coats were worn to the floor, and black boots scuffed the newly polished floors. Brass everywhere was being polished by the crew, and windows were always being washed. There was a stream of people who were pushing and shoving.

Marcus was quite a large and lanky fellow who towered over people. He always considered himself a very plain-looking fellow with his bushy eyebrows. He always had Peterson trim them back for him and cut his hair. His hair silvered with the shock of the death of his parents, and the color never returned at such an early age. He would have Peterson cut his hair, never allowing a barber into his life. Most people who knew of Marcus Rudolph only knew of him by reputation, as a self-made millionaire, yet not too many people actually met him.

He was an eccentric, and his shyness stunted his social development, leaving his social life to be what one would call abnormal.

He was always working through brokers of sorts, relaying information and business data so he didn't ever meet those he was doing business. He would channel large sums of money using different banks as a conduit, making his style of banking known only to himself, and his identity, a secret. He would send different people out to do banking business as himself just to make sure that no one would learn of his identity. He kept a very close rein on his servants. Peterson had been used many times to conduct business transactions with people, unbeknownst to them, that they were dealing with an impostor, the servant, not Marcus Rudolph.

Peterson always got a big thrill pulling off the charade. Passing himself off as Marcus Rudolph was a very deep secret that no one would ever believe.

Marcus's parents died when he was thirteen. He was such a dynamic young individual that the servants stayed on from the instructions from the will and out of love for this young man. His parents left him the small country estate and a very comfortable portfolio, including some very rare paintings that were only known to a handful of people. Paintings secretly transported out of Germany and Austria along with some first-edition books.

His parents made the arrangements for his marriage when he was ten years old, and he thought that he would change his mind.

As the years went on, he forgot about the arrangements, and time passed before his years. When his parents died, life had taken on a different view from the eyes of a thirteen-year-old. His existence became so serious, and socializing with the opposite sex became a very unnecessary part of his life. Marcus decided to enhance the drama by going along with this arranged marriage. He knew of no other way to replenish this emptiness that he subconsciously longed to fill. This man knew that it was time to continue his life with a second generation or all his work would go to no one.

There was never any direction from Peterson. After all, he was just the servant. As much as Peterson loved his employer, his room was still in the basement, along with the cook and the other caretakers of the estate. As friendly as their relationship was, he was still the employer of another class. Peterson loved him like a younger brother since their ages were only eleven years apart. Peterson's father was Marcus's father's valet, and because of the closeness, Peterson took over for Marcus.

# Chapter 12

Upon entering the stateroom, one could smell the recently polished brass made ready for inspection by the next occupant of the stateroom. Dark woods adorned the ceiling-to-floor bedroom suite, and velvet wallpaper covered most of the sitting room. Lavish oriental carpets feathered one's footsteps upon the floor. There was a gorgeous chandelier hanging from the ceiling in the dining area, with smaller lanterns abutting the walls with antique pull chains.

The larger containers were put in steerage, and Peterson told the steward to place the smaller boxes in the bedroom. Possibly under the bed, out of the way, or in a separate area.

Marcus then came into the room after the steward left and removed his outer coverings. Peterson was in the bathroom filling up the lavish bath with hot water. He then laid out towels and made the bathroom ready for his employer.

Marcus was ready for a relaxing bath and then wanted to enjoy dinner. The water in the tub was moving in different directions. Maybe this was an indication of what was to come? Marcus sank down into the water and shut his eyes, allowing the hot water to massage his body. With all his money, he was very content to stay at home, and this journey would be the greatest venture for himself. The steam rising from the bath was making him drift further into dream, and his body was finally relaxing. The dinner tray was being delivered to the door, where Peterson received it and then closed the door. From the motion of the ship, the weather had turned, and he hoped that Marcus would be able to eat his dinner without too much swaying. Peterson had to take some extra steps in one direction and pray to find the right footing so as not to slip with the tray.

Peterson was surprised when Marcus came out of the drawing room in a satin smoking jacket so quickly. Marcus realized that he was hungrier than he expected and wished to dine immediately. He placed himself leisurely down in the dining room. "It smells very good, whatever it is. Peterson, after dinner, I want to walk around the top deck, so please bring me my Scottish wool sweater from the trunk."

Peterson followed directions and remained silent as if he knew that Marcus had some troublesome decisions to make. He had seen and witnessed this silence before. Peterson realized that he was to embark upon a new world, but Marcus was giving up everything, and starting a new life with a new wife and her family. It will take some getting used to—the fact that his employer, Marcus Rudolph, was getting married. Peterson was staying on as his private valet. He was hoping that living in America was going to be better than home. Peterson had heard so much about America. He was trying not to seem like a child, himself with the curiosity of a five-year-old.

Dinner was nearing to an end, and Peterson was shocked out of a dreaming state when Marcus's voice bellowed out, "I can't find my boots, Peterson. I need your help." Voices and demands that he had heard for so many years, and yet, he did love this man.

There weren't too many cabins on the top deck of the ship since it was so expensive and most traveled in second class. No one was out walking. The ship was listing to one side and then to the other due to the twenty-foot seas.

Marcus insisted on going out on deck. Peterson couldn't let him go be himself, so he followed at a distance of ten to fifteen feet so he could have his privacy. As a valet, you had to be always aware of your employer's privacy.

# Chapter 13

The waves were foaming and crashing up and over the front deck. It was thrilling to see it. It was difficult to see anything, but whatever it was that was out there seemed to be challenging every footstep. It became extremely hard to maneuver one's footing. The railings were obscured from view. When Peterson reached out for balance, he barely grabbed the column that he was thrown against.

There seemed to be a calling from the front of the ship, and in an instant, panic ran through his veins. The thunderous crashing and pounding of waves hammered the forward portion on the deck. Peterson instinctively knew he was in trouble. But what about Marcus?

Water everywhere, and then there was nothing. Then there was water and foam, and then there was nothing.

His eyes burned from the saltwater, and he was trying to focus ahead. Peterson was staring at nothing. By now, he was completely soaked, and the weight of his wet clothing hampered his forward strides. Each lumbering step brought Peterson closer to the fact that Marcus Rudolph was not there. Panic was pushing Peterson further. Marcus was not there. That calling must have been him. Realization overcame him, and Peterson was trying to grab hold of the next railing. His hands were frozen and bleeding from the enormous grasping he had to endure in order not to be thrown over himself. But he was losing strength. Strength that he needed in order not to end up like Marcus.

The only problem was that he was sliding up over the edge of the railing, now gaping at the wretched sea, ready to engulf him to his death, when one major wave encompassed him and threw him against the wall, which opened the door from the pressure, and continued to throw him down a whole flight of stairs. If the door had not swung open at the very moment, he, too, would have gone over the side.

"Mr. Rudolph, are you all right?" a voice asked. He was dazed and unable to speak. He couldn't believe what had just happened, or was it just a nightmare? His eyes were closed, and yet, he could feel some hands picking him up and carrying him to the cabin and placing him onto the bed. He wasn't sure if the body of water carried him to his watery grave or if someone was just playing a dirty trick.

"Somebody call the doctor!" shouted in the distance, and voices were around him, but Peterson couldn't open his eyes. He drifted into a dreamlike state and thought that Marcus was calling him and he couldn't reach his hand and only their fingertips touched as Marcus drifted down into the raging sea below. Peterson could hear his own voice yelling that he was coming, but nothing was heard in return.

Falling, falling into the abyss below of cold water and darkness, raging foam, and then falling some more.

"Mr. Rudolph, this is Dr. Carter. Are you all right? Can you hear me? Please keep the cold compresses on your head for the swelling and keep his foot raised!"

There seemed to be an urgency coming from this voice, not knowing exactly why. After trying to move, Peterson knew. His ankle shot pain up his leg, and the doctor had to strap it long enough for the mates to carry him down to sick bay. The ship didn't stop rocking, and the rolling of the top decks didn't allow for maneuvering Mr. Rudolph with ease. The doctor had to decide that he would have to reset his ankle here in his room.

"Get me my instruments from sick bay, and I will have to work here on the bed." The man ran as fast as possible. The door swung open, and the memory of what had happened reappeared in his unconsciousness. "Mr. Rudolph, please lay still," commanded the doctor, and with that, Peterson blacked out.

# Chapter 14

The arrangement for the house was in order, and Sir Henry Von Burger was giving out the final instructions for their guest of honor.

Beatrice tried her best to keep anxiety in check. Such an emotional roller coaster was going on inside her. She was a nervous wreck and anticipating her new husband's arrival. She had heard so little except of his wealth, which couldn't amount to half of her families. She was groomed, in all areas, since a small child, as to how she was to behave. Here it was. It was really going to happen.

"Beatrice, this is the day you are about to meet your husband. No matter what you may think right up front, keep your feelings inside until we can discuss them together tonight," instructed her mother. "This marriage is going to be the event of the year and put all the Bostonians on notice. The Von Burgers know how to receive and respond to international affairs with the best of Boston and what it has to offer," Mother finished just as they heard Father calling from outside the house.

The port was always a place where action was happening in every nick and corner. Vendors grabbing at you to buy their wares. Fruits, fish, and large varieties of overseas goods were carried into wooden shacks for the buyers' eyes to view. People bargaining over prices and yelling at them when they turned their backs and walked away. The smells of the port were like no other. Foods from around the world were being cooked for buyers to taste. Flavors new to their tongues. Shoppers would either smile with satisfaction or spit out the food on the ground in disgust.

People from around the world. Some here to sell their traveled goods, others here to start a new life in America. What were the hopes and dreams that drove people to travel the oceans of the world? The yearnings for a better life in America? Using America as a stop-over for business? Whatever their reasons were, it was here for their own self-discovery. The pulse of the port could be felt for miles and miles. Travelers came from all directions.

Beatrice felt the overwhelming desire to flee, run away. No matter how much preparation there had been for this day, she wasn't able to control herself. She was about to meet the man she would spend the rest of her life with, and everyone around her was so casual about the event.

The driver was hampered by all the people meandering in the streets. The pushcarts were too heavy laden with enormous loads of goods to sell. The vendors were moving too slow.

"Get out of our way, you slowpoke!" shouted Sir Henry Von Burger, pointing to one man.

He shoved his head out the door to yell when a hand came out of nowhere and grabbed his hat. "Stop!" he yelled. It was too late. The two men were too far in the opposite direction. "No one does that to me, those bastards. I'll catch them." He then demanded faster traveling if they were to be at the right dock on time.

All this had really put her into a state of extreme physical fatigue. Father wouldn't stop about his hat. The dust and dirt from the streets made a layer of soot upon their clothing, shoes, and skin. Beatrice could feel her throat narrowing from her nerves. She was resting her eyes closed, and no matter how brightly the sun was shining, she felt the clouds of doom upon her. Beatrice mentally braced herself against the street life of reckless dimension or her family's control, she floated into a state of withdrawal. Beatrice learned this at a very early age when she needed more self-control. It was her hideaway.

# Chapter 15

The pushing and pulling was amazing. No one could go anywhere. Beatrice couldn't understand why there was so much confusion. Ropes were everywhere so people couldn't get too close to the edge of the dock.

Sir Henry Von Burger had the driver park elsewhere after dropping them off as close to the pier as possible. The *Summerfest* was in, and their anticipation of a new member to the family was overwhelming, even for Sir Henry Von Burger. His daughter was going to marry a young man from the blue bloods of Europe. Boston was going to be put on their heels. Their wedding will be the event of the century. There on the dock, Sir Henry Von Burger and his wife stood and waited for their new son-in-law. Beatrice waited for her new husband. And they waited and waited.

People came out of the small door atop the bridge and fumbled down the gangplank. They watched women struggling with their small children, warning them to hold securely to the railings. Men were carrying more than they could handle. Sir Henry Von Burger never saw so many valises, trunks, and crates. He was still very upset about his hat. Most people were off the ship when, in the distance, Henry could see a man being helped from the storage compartment near the end of the ship. His wheelchair was stuck in what seemed to be some cracks, and the stewards, he thought, were carrying him down the walkway in the chair. All the luggage was piled high, and the man disappeared behind a wall of trunks.

After two hours of watching and waiting, Sir Henry Von Burger was about to blow his stack. He was pacing back and forth, making everyone in his path move aside. Beatrice was in tears and sitting on some crate found near a pole. The temperature turned quite cold, and the harbor winds started picking up. They were beginning to realize that Marcus Rudolph wasn't there.

"Excuse me, sir." Some man was pulling at Sir Von Burger's shirt sleeve.

He turned around and saw this dirty man with a note. He handed it to him and waited for some sort of tip, but it never came. The man left the dock mumbling something about what a cheap bastard he was. Sir Henry Von Burger opened the note to read, "There has been an accident on board the ship, and Mr. Marcus Rudolph has disembarked from the stern portion of the ship. He is in a wheelchair waiting for you at the end of the dock. Signed, the Doctor."

With the greatest of speed, Sir Henry Von Burger, his wife, and Beatrice ran to where Henry thought he saw this man being helped earlier off the ship. The weather really turned nasty, and Beatrice's bonnet came loose, and if not for the ribbon under the chin holding it to her body, it would have blown away. Even though she was running in one direction, the wind was pushing her backward in the opposite direction. Perhaps fate was telling her something: "Turn yourself around, child, for this man will bring only disaster." But her thoughts all changed when she saw him.

Marcus Rudolph was sitting in a wheelchair all bundled up against now the stormy weather cutting through their bones. His head had a white bandage completely wrapped around covering his eyebrows. One side came down over his ear and then around his neck. You couldn't really see much of his face except his eyes. Beatrice became paralyzed with fear yet, reached out for his frozen hand on the side.

She then saw his leg straight out in front of him. It, too, had been placed in a cast to keep it secure. What happened to him? Her mind went out of control, and she started screaming at the man standing next to him. The steward started to explain when Marcus Rudolph dismissed him and summoned Sir Henry Von Burger.

"Shall we go? We'll talk later."

With those instructions, they were all at his beck and call. Sir Henry Von Burger thought he couldn't believe the condition of his new son-in-law. What a mess. What happened? His mind went crazy. The driver was signaled to come and pick them up with extra help for all the added luggage, crates, and trunks.

# Chapter 16

Beatrice sat back resting her head staring at a man who was about to become her husband. What kind of a man was he? her mind wondered. It felt so good just to be in the inside, where the wind couldn't bite at her body anymore. They were all cramped into a small space, leaving Marcus's leg room to rest with the cast.

Conversation didn't start until Sir Henry Von Burger broke the silence. "Whatever did happen to you while on board? Were you mugged? Were you in a fight?" questioned Henry.

Marcus hardly opened his eyes when he spoke. "I was walking around the deck. The weather was getting very bad, but I didn't realize how bad. I opened the door to get in, and a large wall of water carried me through the door and tossed me down a flight of stairs. One of the stewards found me and called for help. I don't remember anything except the water picking me up and playing with me. Thank God I was pushed in the right direction. I might have been tossed overboard. I am dreadfully sorry for my appearance, Beatrice. I am very sorry."

She blushed uncontrollably, and she already found this man rather intriguing. Beatrice bowed her chin, showing approval and acceptance. He was very polite and very polished. She thought that her father would like that very much. He spoke perfect English except a small accent, which she found most exciting. He, of course, looked much older than she expected, but with all that had happened, that was understandable. His wounds would heal, and the real Marcus Rudolph would appear. So far, she approved of the family's decision. She closed her eyes and proceeded to go over the next year of events planned out to perfection. The gifts, the showers, the courtship with this man. She would be dressed in a beautiful white wedding gown on her special day. The perfect day. All this was really going to happen. Life was going to be wonderful.

*Chapter 17*

Samantha was on the phone with Reliable Investigators the minute she arrived at home. Mr. Phillips was very understanding since he had done work for the family before. There would be files to go through and people to be paid off. He promised to get the job done as soon as possible and reveal his information to no one except her.

"You must keep all information to yourself. Please do not let my father know that you are working for me. I don't want anyone to know that I am looking for my mother. You are not to speak to my father about anything. Is that understood?" Samantha demanded a verbal answer since she couldn't really believe that she was really doing this.

She now had to know the woman who gave her life. Now she understood the coolness or aloofness she felt all these years from her mother Beatrice. She never felt the warmth and always felt that she did something wrong. It wasn't her. It was her father's wrongdoing.

She was going to have to pull herself together and not mention this to anyone. She told Mr. Phillips to put someone on her husband and watch him like a hawk. She was tired of being lied to. Not anymore. Not to Samantha Arpel.

# Chapter 18

Katherine planned on a 10:00 a.m. doctor's appointment today for her yearly checkup, but the doctor was running late. She was annoyed. So much to do at work. Katherine knew that it was a mistake to take this time off from work but was compelled to make and keep this appointment.

At least Dr. Myers's office wasn't the typical cold and impersonal office. He had beautiful pictures of all sizes on one whole wall. All his pictures were photographs of the scenic scope. All done in black and white. The details were excellent. Then she noticed his signature at the bottom of all of them. She was shocked at the depth he caught in such detail view through the eyes of the camera. It was another side of Dr. Myers that made his patients feel more in touch with him. Katherine really didn't think of him as anything else other than a doctor. The nurse then called her name and was directed back to the examining room. Katherine undressed and put the usual robe on just as the doctor came in.

"Good morning, Katherine, how are you feeling?"

Katherine was finally there, so she might as well let it all out. Katherine started, "I'm fine. I just find it hard for me to stay asleep in the morning beyond five o'clock. I guess that's normal sometimes. I haven't been feeling right for about a month. I seem to get agitated easily, and my headaches that I get seem to be getting worse."

Katherine said it and felt ridiculous because there she sat now feeling better. "OK, now it's time to leave," she thought.

Dr. Myers told Katherine to hold her arms out straight and point her fingers for a little test. He checked her coordination and did his usual things that doctors do. He poked and prodded and walked around to her back. Hands were traveling all over her. Her mind was trying to search for whatever his fingers were trained to do.

"How long do the headaches last, and how do they come on?" He asked.

"They start with a sharp pinpoint like shooting stab and travel from the right eye to the back of my head on the same side." Katherine answered with more concern and wondered what he wanted or what he was looking for. She was starting to really worry by his expression across his face.

"There are some tests that I want to run, and we'll do them tomorrow at 10:00 a.m. I don't need excuses why you can't be there, so don't even start with me. My nurse will do the regular preliminary procedures, and be a good girl, don't give her any trouble."

With that little-girl speech, Dr. Myers tapped Katherine on the cheek with his knuckles and walked out the door. "My god, what is he looking for?"

Katherine could feel the flush of anxiety rush over her, and she decided to behave herself. If it weren't for the nausea that she felt, she might have started to chuckle. After all, she felt fine upon entering his office, and with this kind of fright, her senses were now working overtime.

Jonathan was working in his office when a calm, yet, panicky voice came over the phone. "What's the matter?" Jonathan could feel the instant sweat and clammy fingers holding the receiver. "Katherine, are you all right?"

"I'm all right now, now that I have you on the phone. I want to see you later. I miss you, and I've decided not to come in today. Dr. Myers wants to do some tests tomorrow, and to tell you the truth, I feel a little scared." Katherine took a breath and went on. "Any chance of us getting together tonight?"

"Of course, my darling. I'm coming over right now. Don't go anywhere."

Katherine added with relief, "No, I have something to do. Please come over later, and I'll make dinner."

"I don't care who sees me. I can't stand being away from you, and if something is wrong, I want to be at your side."

With that, Jonathan hung up.

Katherine was trying not to turn herself into a nervous wreck but just thinking about what the doctor was referring to, with all these upcoming tests for tomorrow, didn't make her feel at ease. All she wanted was her mother and grandmother with her.

# Chapter 19

**M**r. Phillips was almost out of breath when he finished climbing the staircase. The shabby house known to so many women in those days hadn't changed in all these years. He was about to knock on the tattered door when it opened.

"Hello, what do you want here?" asked an old weather-beaten-faced woman, barely able to stand up straight herself.

"I was supposed to see Angel. I called. I need some information about a lady of some years ago. Is she in?"

"You spoke to me. I'm Angel. Come on in." Angel opened the door.

He then wanted to jump out of his skin when he entered the house. The stench reeked of old mold and mildew that encrusted him, and he couldn't wait to hightail it out of there. The thought of what went on here made him sick.

He didn't know where to sit, so he stood there and watched this fragile piece of structure maneuver herself to what must have been her favorite chair. The odor, oh my. He thought he must get out of here as quickly as possible.

He started to ask his questions. This poor old lady's mind was much better than her appearance, and his interview with her was more successful than imaginable.

"I know that many years ago, this house was used to console women who were having babies out of wedlock and satisfy their male counterparts," Mr. Phillips continued. "Do you keep records of those ladies? And if you do, I need to know about one particular one named Mary. She worked for the Rudolphs."

Angel's face went paste white. She knew that someday this would come to pass. She had hoped that these questions wouldn't get her into trouble.

"I have never kept records because all my girls are in my head. In this business, you never write anything down 'cause it will be held against you." She paused. "Mary worked for the Rudolphs for a few years and then got in trouble. I was not supposed to know who the father was, but I always figured it out, and besides, the girls would always end up telling me. I always looked out for my girls." With that, she stopped talking, and she grabbed her chest.

"Oh my god, she's the one." Remnants of memory flashed by for Angel. She sat straight up.

Mr. Phillips thought that she was having a heart attack, but she wasn't. He moved quickly over to her, and that was when Angel looked up at him and said, "Don't ask me any more questions. I can't remember anything else about Mary. Please go!"

He straightened Angel up on the chair, now in a slumped position, and continued on, as if not hearing her request. She started to tap her fingers on the arms of the chair and twist her feet around the legs. He thought, "How weird."

As he pumped her for more information, her tongue became more fluid with the money crossing her palms. He was given incredible information that would embarrass Mr. Marcus Rudolph himself, never mind Samantha. Mr. Phillips was already talking to himself. All he could think of was how Samantha was going to accept this information. There was going to be a family collision causing such a trauma that it could paralyze not just the family but the whole community when this information got out. He knew that he held information about the most aristocratic and prosperous family in the city. It was about to be scandalized. Could Samantha hold up to the impact of information that will change her life forever?

Leads had to be followed up and confirmed. He couldn't believe that Sir Henry Von Burger was involved. As he exited this mangy house, he tore his right shirt sleeve on a nail sticking out from the doorframe, producing a small trace of blood. He didn't even stop to grab the cut with his other hand. His mind was on too many other things. So much to do. His thoughts were wheeling with information, and contacts had to be made. He himself was in disbelief. This old lady. How could she? Traces of the stench were still in his nostrils. He had to get out for some fresh air. "What was she thinking back then?" his mind wondered. He had to get back to his office and put some calls to the Midwest before the time change.

He got back to his office with all his notes and couldn't believe that his first interview was right on target. It was only six days since they talked. He didn't want to call Samantha just yet, but her message was already on his message machine.

"Is Samantha there, please?" he asked.

"Who's this?" asked Jonathan.

"This is Mr. Phelps. I'm working on the horticultural yearly fundraiser. Is this her husband?"

"Yes, it is. I'll get her. Sam!" he yelled.

"Hi, Mrs. Arpel, Samantha. Don't talk, just listen. I told your husband that I was Mr. Phelps helping you on the horticultural fundraiser." He paused. "I've got some inconceivable information for you, but not over the phone. I want you at my office tomorrow at 10:30 a.m., and we can proceed depending on what you want me to do." With that, they both hung up.

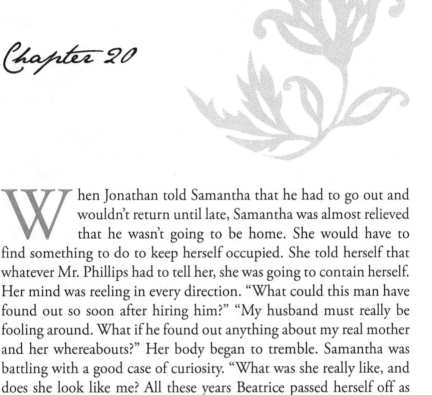

# Chapter 20

When Jonathan told Samantha that he had to go out and wouldn't return until late, Samantha was almost relieved that he wasn't going to be home. She would have to find something to do to keep herself occupied. She told herself that whatever Mr. Phillips had to tell her, she was going to contain herself. Her mind was reeling in every direction. "What could this man have found out so soon after hiring him?" "My husband must really be fooling around. What if he found out anything about my real mother and her whereabouts?" Her body began to tremble. Samantha was battling with a good case of curiosity. "What was she really like, and does she look like me? All these years Beatrice passed herself off as my mother. She should have told me about what happened or stayed in touch with Mary after she left town," Samantha thought. "Why didn't Mary ever get in touch with me?" So many questions. "Oh, Mr. Phillips, why didn't you call earlier so we could talk tonight?" Samantha was talking to herself out loud, and it felt good. "I'm so glad Jonathan isn't here."

Jonathan had to reach Katherine as soon as possible, and he almost didn't care who knew about his love for her. Samantha seemed to be so busy with all her fundraisers that he felt that it was keeping her out of his way. She got so tied up with the responsibilities there wasn't any time for him. He reached her house and parked outside for the world to see. He didn't care. She was waiting by the door when he came to ring the bell. Katherine buried her head into his shoulder and sobbed out of frustration and fear.

"I am going into the hospital for some tests tomorrow. I only plan on staying a couple of days. I'll be giving my workload to Liz until I come back." Katherine gasped for air.

Jonathan didn't want to talk anymore. He was only interested in making Katherine comfortable and getting her thoughts on something else. "My darling, I love you with all my heart, and I want to make you happy tonight."

Katherine couldn't believe that he was actually in her house. "Jonathan, what would happen if Samantha found out about us?"

"Katherine, don't worry about such matters now. I'm not letting you go through these tests alone. I'll be there for you. No matter what."

Jonathan poured himself a strong cocktail and some wine for Katherine. The table was set, and yet they sat on the sofa in silence waiting for time to pass. Music filled the room. Both were drawing solace from each other. Silence was the best remedy. Too much talk would set a plateau of real worry. So here they sat in silence, in this beautiful home, which was the very first time Jonathan was there. He sat there studying all the wall decorations and old pictures, books, and antiques placed around the room. If he had to picture her house, it would be just like this. Katherine displayed old family pictures on the mantelpiece over the roaring fire. It was perfect, except what was wrong with his Katherine?

# Chapter 21

T hank God for sleeping pills. Samantha wasn't going to take any chances not sleeping. These pills didn't leave her in a state of confusion. She needed a clear head to deal with Mr. Phillips today. She didn't even care what time Jonathan came in last night.

The morning wasn't going fast enough for her, so she got dressed in her usual slacks and a baggy sweatshirt. "What could he have found out so soon?" was on her mind, and her curiosity was piqued? What did her husband do last night? "Wow. Am I going to catch him in some relationship with another woman?" Samantha's mind was flying with steamy thoughts.

Mr. Phillips was seated at his desk with a fresh cup of coffee. You could smell the pot brewing from the elevator door down the hall.

"Samantha, sit down. Would you like some coffee?" He got up to pour some into a mug, not waiting for her reply.

"No."

"What do you put in it?"

Samantha's heart started to race with each fleeting moment and braced herself at the edge of the wooded armchair. She thought about the back of the chair being so straight and strong. She needed it right now.

"What I'm about to tell you is going to change your life forever. What you choose to do with this information is totally up to you. Your mother has already turned your whole world upside down. You must decide if you want to pursue further into my investigation of your mother."

Samantha sat there without saying a word. She nodded, affirmative.

Phillips continued, "When you told me about your search for your real mother, I made some calls but didn't know exactly where my leads would direct me. I found a woman named Angel. She took care of young girls who had babies out of wedlock. Angel used to run a house many years ago where men sent their pregnant lovers, girlfriends, mistresses to have their babies or abort them.

"Samantha, Angel told me that there was a girl by the name of Mary who worked for your family. She was from Ireland and had no place to go when she came to this county. She came to this country and had to find work. The only thing she could do is clean houses for the rich."

Samantha sat there knowing this information from Beatrice. So far, she wasn't too impressed, so she drank her coffee without interrupting.

"Your father, after ten years of Mary's employment, took her in a way that would be very embarrassing, if you know what I mean. Mary told everybody that is was a cook down the street, but out of respect for your father, people only talked elsewhere. Your mother understood that men get crazy sometimes and things like this happen. Beatrice was known around town as being very cold to Marcus. He had made it known. So he looked to Mary to warm his bed."

Samantha was still waiting for some information about her mother and her whereabouts. She was getting very frustrated listening to Phillips.

"Go on, please," she insisted.

"I spoke to Angel for quite a while. What she insisted on telling me was, that she and Mary, were the only ones that knew what really happened."

Samantha was feeling a little weak by now.

Phillips had to get it off his chest, so he just blurted it out, "Samantha, there were two fetuses, two babies born. A set of twin girls were born to Mary." He hesitated and then went on. "You have a twin sister, Samantha. Mary made Angel promise never to tell anyone cause Mr. Marcus Rudolph would want both."

He then continued to quote Angel. "The wealthy always get what they want, and he is not getting this one, too. She insisted. Mary pleaded with such passion that Angel couldn't break her heart any more than it was already. Mary was going to have to choose which baby to keep and which one to give to Mr. Marcus Rudolph. Angel promised to keep their secret. Mary, then had to make her choice. She wanted one of these babies more than ever. She had to hide it from Marcus. Angel thought that Mary was such a pitiful child. She had to help her. After all, Marcus Rudolph was getting to bring up his child, you, Samantha. Beatrice went away for a few months and came back with you. People and friends believed that she gave birth to you while visiting family elsewhere." Phillips was exhausted from Angel's confession.

Samantha got out of her chair, walked around the office, and looked out of the window with her cup of coffee.

"And here I thought you found my husband in the arms of another woman. Now, you tell me about my mother having twins? I can't believe it. I just can't believe it. I have a twin sister. I have family I never met. A mother that I've never met." Samantha stood just looking out the window.

Mr. Phillips finally got out of his chair and took Samantha by the shoulder and walked her over to the sofa and sat her down.

"Samantha, I hope that you can pull yourself together. We have a lot to do to follow-up on this. How do you feel?" He waited. "Samantha, are you all right?"

"Yes, I'm all right. I just have to let all this sink in. You're telling me that all my life that I've had a twin sister, and even my father didn't know about twins being born. What a joke on him. That bastard! My poor mother, I mean, my real mother. She must have gone through hell." Samantha got very annoyed. "Where is she? We have to find my sister!" Samantha's face was dripping in tears. She could feel a tremendous pulling of her nervous system and found herself pacing the floor. There was an urgency to find her sister.

"What does she look like? Does she look like me being a twin? I can't wait. Do you think, Mr. Phillips, that she knows about me? Of course you don't know." Samantha was now rambling on to herself. "I can't believe it," she mumbled and again, sat down on that straight-backed wooden chair.

Phillips thought that she took the news pretty well, considering. "She must have an emotional structure of a lion." Samantha was going to be all right, and he felt very good about telling her. Now they both knew that they must go on into this investigation, wherever it would lead. Phillips answered the ringing phone.

"Samantha Arpel is here with me now. What information did you pick up from your connection?" Samantha listened. "How did you know where to look? Are sure about this? Do you know if we could? Don't worry about the money, I'll get some more to you. Just get back to that rooming house. Pay whatever it takes to find them." Phillips hung up the phone.

"Samantha, I placed calls to some friends yesterday, out of state. Are you ready?" Without waiting for a reply, he continued, "It seems that your grandfather Sir Henry Von Burger set the whole thing up with Angel and transferred Mary and the baby to his furniture factory in Iowa."

Samantha couldn't believe all this was happening. What a revelation. Now she could put together all those moments when she didn't feel like part of the family. Beatrice used to give her a look of hate, and for what? What did she ever do? Never any hugs. Never time spent together growing up. Her father always too busy working or whatever he did. Now, all the pieces were beginning to fit into place.

Samantha wasn't imagining it about her mother's lack of affection. Her grandfather stole her sister and mother away, not even telling her father about twins being born. "How ruthless. I'm glad his is dead. I'm glad that I never cried at my grandfather's funeral. In fact, not too many other people did either. I hate him. Why did he do this to me, to her? To my mother? To Beatrice?"

# Chapter 22

Katherine was feeling very weak from the morning testing but had to complete a couple more tests later. The nurses were very nice and very impressed that she was Dr. Myer's patient. He turned out to be head of his department. She had a private room so Jonathan could visit anytime. Because of the test, she wasn't able to eat earlier and was starving.

"How about some soup or Jell-O, nurse?" she asked. Jonathan just walked in. Katherine's face began to glow.

"Hello, darling, these are for you." He gave her two dozen yellow roses. Her favorites. Just then, another nurse came in and told them that Katherine was scheduled now for a CAT scan. Jonathan had to wait for her in her room.

"My darling, I'll be right here. I'm not leaving this hospital until you leave."

Katherine couldn't believe this wonderful man she so loved. Jonathan made some phone calls when Katherine was in testing.

"Jacob, if Samantha calls, tell her I'm in meetings most of the day and I will call her back. Anyone else, tell them that I went on a trip for a couple of days and will call back. Call me if there is an emergency at the mill." He then hung up.

Time seemed to pass so slowly when you're waiting for medical information. He had done so many business deals, but he was the one who always kept people waiting. When to buy, when to sell or leave it alone. Brokers to convince that timing was right or wrong. Now, here he sat, waiting for somebody else to call the shots. Dr. Myers said he would come out and tell them together. Hours had passed just when Jonathan saw Dr. Myers walking with another doctor. Dr. Myers looked at Jonathan and escorted him to a small office at the end of the corridor. Jonathan followed the two doctors. There was such silence. Such tension.

"Jonathan, this is Dr. Kent, our head of Obstetrics of the hospital." They shook hands, and Dr. Myers went on. "We have some very serious information that you should listen to. Now sit down." They all sat around a table.

"Excuse me, Dr. Myers, I thought that you were going to discuss whatever with both of us? Why just me?"

Dr. Kent interrupted, "Jonathan, there are some things that have to be discussed in the best interest for Katherine. We were hoping to talk to you first so you could help us later."

Jonathan could feel his sweat glands go into overtime and the temperature in the room went up to what seemed like one hundred degrees.

"First, congratulations, Katherine is about two months pregnant."

Jonathan thought he said that Katherine was pregnant but wasn't quite sure. Jonathan had to interrupt. "Did you say that Katherine is pregnant, Doctor?" Jonathan repeated the statement, or was it a question?

"Yes, Katherine is two months pregnant."

Jonathan was so shocked. He always wanted to have a baby with Samantha, but she always wanted to put it off till later. She always had excuses. Now Katherine and he were going to have a baby. How wonderful.

"Mr. Arpel, Jonathan, are you listening to me? There are some other factors that you need to know for the health of Katherine." The doctors looked at each other with frustration written all over their faces. "It doesn't look good for the continuation of this pregnancy. Just so we don't get too technical, we'll put it into layman's terms. We found a large tumor lodged in an area of Katherine's brain that cannot be operated on. Being pregnant is highly dangerous for Katherine's health and the baby. We can try chemo to decrease the size of the tumor, but not while she's pregnant. The pregnancy puts too much pressure on her body functions, raising her blood pressure, and a good chance that the tumor would grow at an increased speed. Her blood pressure can rise, and she could hemorrhage. We can't control all the variables going on in her body and the growth of the baby."

"Jonathan, we need your help. We have to convince Katherine to abort this child. We cannot wait days, weeks, or months to treat this tumor. There is too much at risk. If we treat her for the tumor, then the baby will be abnormal in too many ways to even mention. She can always have other babies. Jonathan, it is imperative that she aborts." Dr. Kent placed his hand on Jonathan's shoulder to try to impress the importance of this decision.

Bent over like an old man with his elbows balanced on the top portion of his legs, his head in his hands, Jonathan wanted to scream. Beads of sweat continued to cover his face and his shaking hands were out of control. His mind was trying to remember everything the doctors just said to him. He remembered the stabbing pain of being told that his parents died in an auto crash. The feeling of loss was washing all over his body.

He asked himself, "What did I do to deserve this? Why did my parents die so young?" It was all coming back now. His rage was taking over his body, and he couldn't stop shaking. His parents, his Katherine, and now his baby. "Dear God, when does it stop? When does the pain stop? What did I do to deserve this? Oh, my heart is breaking, and I can't do anything about it. I feel so helplessness again." His mind was so deep in a trace, and his body was so statue-like.

"Jonathan? Jonathan?" Dr. Myers was trying to get him to acknowledge them. Both doctors carefully moved Jonathan into another chair and whispered his name again. Jonathan reacted with a jolt. They continued.

"Katherine has to be told. We'll all be there. She has to abort as soon as possible. We have to start chemotherapy right away," Dr.

Kent insisted. "I'll be back in two hours, and Katherine should be back in her room. Let's plan on it then. Agreed?"

The doctors walked out of the conference room, leaving Jonathan alone with nothing but the last words he could recall. "She has to abort. She cannot have this baby, but there will be others. We have to convince her."

This couldn't be happening. How was he going to convince her to do what these doctors were asking, insisting? He himself wanted this baby. He wanted this baby more than anything. He couldn't believe that Katherine was having a baby, his baby. "My baby," there, he said it out loud. "Katherine could die. I can't let her die. She must have the abortion!" He felt this large pit in the bottom of his stomach and didn't know where to go until Katherine was scheduled back in her room. He decided to go back to the office, but only got as far as his car, where he stretched his arms across the steering wheel and cried like a baby.

# Chapter 23

Samantha got home late in the afternoon. With trembling hands, she poured herself a drink in the study. She never spent much time in this room since it was really Jonathan's. She was going over and over all the information Mr. Phillips gave her. She sat there looking out onto the back gardens, letting the stiff alcohol take its effect over her body. Her head was spinning. She couldn't do anything except burst into an uncontrollable sobbing frenzy. Samantha's tears flowed for herself, for her mother, for her sister. Her body was wrenched over the overstuffed chair sobbing when the phone rang.

"Oh, let it ring," she said. "Oh my god, what if it's Mr. Phillips?" Samantha ran and cleared her voice before picking up the receiver. "Hello?" It was barely a whisper. "Hello, Samantha, this is Jacob. I'm calling just to let you know that Jonathan won't be home tonight. He had an emergency with one of the mills in New Hampshire and had to fly up this afternoon. He tried calling you, but you weren't anywhere to be found. Is everything all right? He'll call you later." She then hung up without saying anything.

Her mind went to Phillips. She had to find out some information about her husband. She was going to find out what was going on with his life. They had not been together as husband and wife for some time. She didn't know where or when the communications failed between them. She knew that someone else was in his life. She could feel it. She would have to handle that too when the time came.

Emotional fatigue was now taking over her body with a combination of the two drinks she made for herself. Samantha decided to take a warm bath and go to bed. She didn't want to think anymore. She wanted to block out everything right now. She couldn't turn her brain off. She started tormenting herself. All she could think about was her mother. "She had to make a choice. 'Which baby should I keep?' Why couldn't she have chosen me? What a horrible thing for a mother to have to do. Why did she give me to my father when I could have known her all my life? Now she remains a mystery to me." Samantha's body was floating in hot water and her mind floating in alcohol.

"Please, I want to go to sleep." She was screaming out loud to this empty bathroom. Her body was numb, and her mind was in too much pain to continue today. Oh, much too much pain. With the information learned today, how would she get through the tomorrows?

# Chapter 24

Jonathan tried to get something to eat in the cafeteria before going upstairs, but nothing attracted his appetite. Nerves were frayed. In the men's room, he washed up. He was going to have to be very strong for Katherine.

He was going to be as casual as possible. "How's my love?" He grabbed Katherine with full force and wrapped his arms of iron around her.

"I've been waiting for you. Where have you been? They're going to come in here and tell us the results. Then, we can get the hell out of here." Katherine was obviously very cranky from not eating all day. Maybe it was the aftermath from the tests. Jonathan knew that it was going to be a real battle, and he had to keep up the front.

"I see the two of you are here," Dr. Myers blurted out, followed by Dr. Kent. He then closed the door behind them.

Katherine looked puzzled but kept quiet. Her senses started to overreact and knew something was wrong when a strange doctor came in. Dr. Myers took the chair from the other side of the room and placed it directly in front of the bed. Jonathan had to move his legs, which were hanging over to one side of the bed. Jonathan's body was balancing at the edge and had to move more into the center. Katherine thought, "How cozy. Here we are, all four, facing each other. Now what?"

"Katherine, this is Dr. Kent. I called him into the picture of things since we all need some expert advice. Dr. Kent is a specialist in ob-gyn. It seems, young lady," he took Katherine's other hand, "you are pregnant, two months pregnant." They all nodded to one another, confirming the statement.

"So why do you all look so serious? Is there something wrong with my baby?" Katherine just realized what she said. "My baby. Wow!" She looked into Jonathan's eyes looking for some reaction to all this. "What's wrong? Jonathan, how come you know already?" By now she was moving all over the bed.

"Katherine, calm down. The baby is fine. It's not the baby. Tests show that there is a problem with you." There, he said it. Jonathan continued, "It would be very dangerous for you to continue on with this pregnancy."

"Jonathan, are you telling me that there is something wrong with me and I can't have this baby? What is so terrible with me that I can't have this baby? Your baby, Jonathan? Are you all crazy? Of course I am having this baby. This is my baby, and I will have it." Katherine was kneeling on the bed pleading with the two male doctors shaking their heads.

Dr. Myers took over, "Please try to understand something, Katherine. All of the tests show that at the bottom of your skull, there is a large tumor. This tumor has been causing your headaches and your irritability for some time. I don't believe you told anybody about them until recently. The tumor must come out, and we cannot operate on it. It's in the worst possible position of the skull. If we do operate, Katherine, you would be a vegetable for life, or worst, die. We want to treat it with chemotherapy, but you cannot be pregnant. Your baby will get all the radiation, and that will cause deformities or kill her."

"Oh my god," Katherine was rambling. "It's a she. She now knows the sex, a girl. She's really a person, and I'm going to have a baby girl. How wonderful!" Katherine's eyes were traveling from one doctor to the other, and then to Jonathan, and then back to the first doctor. She was convincing them that she was having this child.

"Nobody is taking my baby from me. I am having this baby, and I will have to take my chances on getting better. I won't do anything to harm my baby, and I will have her. I will stay in bed, do whatever you tell me. I am having this baby. This is the most wonderful thing that has ever happened to me, and you are not ending my pregnancy. Is that understood?" Katherine's eyes were now on fire, and all three men decided to leave Katherine alone for a while. She was upset enough.

Jonathan, all of a sudden, became the enemy too. He was trying to be on the doctors' side when, he, too, wanted this baby, but not at the cost of Katherine's life. He didn't want to upset her any more than she already was, so he left the room with the doctors. "Please get some rest now, and I'll be right back to sit with you, honey." Jonathan patted her on the head like a little girl, which infuriated her.

Outside the room, Dr. Myers said, "Jonathan, you must convince her what's right for her. We'll keep her in the hospital a couple of days, and let's begin treatment after aborting. We can treat her as an outpatient, and treatment will take, hopefully, about two months. If we see some improvement in the tumor sooner, then it might be a shorter time frame." Dr. Myers shook his head. After leaving, Jonathan went back into see Katherine.

"Before you start with me, I want to say something. I am having this baby, your baby, our baby, and that's it. I don't want to start talking about my health and what might be. I am going to having our daughter. I've already given her the name of my mother. I don't want to discuss anything anymore, or we will not speak again."

Jonathan was so taken back by Katherine's attitude. They couldn't even discuss it. Was this the woman whom he loved? He didn't want to lose her to death or live without her and their child. While he was in his own turmoil, he didn't realize that Katherine was packing up her belongings since there wasn't any reason to stay in the hospital. By the time he turned around, she was walking in front of the nurses' station waving goodbye. She was leaving without permission.

"You can't just leave!" shouted the head nurse, racing for the phone.

"Babies were born for centuries without you and your hospitals. So shall mine. I'm having this child, and nobody will tell me otherwise." Katherine had to find sanctuary with someone who would understand completely. She had to get out of the hospital before any harm came to her baby. She knew actually where she had to go, and it didn't include Jonathan or anybody but herself and her baby. She had to get out, and panic was threatening her life with every step.

Katherine escaped down the stairs followed by Jonathan helping her with the doors. He brought her to the bottom and said that he would help her in any way he could. He was not about to lose her. He was already at a loss. A loss of his mind. He was a married man and having a child with another woman. He really was at a loss.

Katherine needed to rest. She insisted that he drop her off at home and promised to get some sleep. She had a lot of thinking and would call him later. Her mind was made up, and after her nap, she had things to do. She was going to handle everything. Everything was going to be just fine.

# Chapter 25

Mr. Phillips thought that he had a man watching Jonathan. He was supposed to report all activities every few hours to Phillips, except he couldn't find him. "Great!" thought Phillips. Jonathan's office said that he went away for a few days. It didn't make him look too good. "Losing your client's husband on the first day. What a mess. Where could he be?" He didn't want to ask Samantha. After all, he was supposed to be the investigator. He didn't know that Samantha was told that he was in New Hampshire straightening out business matters.

Phillip's day was already planned. He was taking a plane to Iowa and seeing for himself the factory that Sir Henry Von Burger established. The factory that created this dynasty of deception. Information he received forced him to make sure that it was correct. He was a very thorough investigator, and he didn't want any screw-ups. His resources sometimes exaggerate information just to make it seem that they were doing a better job than they really were. He wasn't going to look like an idiot to Mrs. Samantha Arpel. This was too important.

"Samantha, you will have to wait until I call you later with more information. I am going out to Iowa on some info received. I must go, my plane is waiting. If I need you, I know where to find you. We'll talk about your husband later." Phillips struggled to get off the phone.

It was already late afternoon, and Samantha was beginning to show signs of stress. She wanted to pick up the phone and call her father and get to the bottom of this but didn't want to do that until she heard from Phillips. What was she going to do with herself? Samantha was in such shock over the information learned about her real identity. She couldn't even talk about it with Jonathan. Jonathan would never believe it. In fact, nobody would believe this. She was so embarrassed about it. Just think, you were not who you think you were. All these years, and she was living with a woman who wasn't her real mother. It was unthinkable. It was hard enough getting through yesterday. How was she going to get through today? Samantha couldn't stop talking to herself and shaking her head in disbelief. She tried to make something to eat for herself. As she fumbled around the kitchen holding onto the counters, she felt like she was about to throw up.

"Who am I? What is she really like?" Her mother must have wondered the same questions. "Why didn't she just come for me since she knew where I was all along?" Her head began to spin again, and the pounding wouldn't quit. Samantha never took drugs to get rid of hangovers. What was it? Samantha just sat there gazing out onto the backyard. "I know I can't sit here all day. I'll go out of my mind." She was thankful that the house was empty and she had the freedom to speak out loud without anyone there. Samantha was torturing herself, shielding her face in her hands, when she all of a sudden knew the answer. "Oh my god, I'll go to see Fr. Ryan. I'll go see him. I can't stay here. He'll help me."

Samantha hadn't been to church in years, but she always did find comfort there. She always enjoyed his sermons. Samantha decided that she really needed to talk to someone. Fr. Ryan, of course. He was the only person she could share this with and knew that it wouldn't go any further. She ran upstairs to dress when she saw all those mirrors in her room staring back at her. Samantha walked very slowing up to one mirror and placed her full hand on its reflection. "Who am I? Where is my mother and sister?" It was some time before she stopped crying and dragged herself to the shower stall. "I am going to find out everything."

While Samantha finished getting dressed, she remembered that she had her old Bible in the dining room. She unlocked the glass bookcase and picked it up with the greatest of care. It was a treasured Bible that had been in the family for generations. The black leather binding was quite worn. There was the family crest embossed, in gold, on the cover with a gold trim around the corners of each edge. Inside was the inscription, "With this book, you will find your way, Henry." Her parents had given this Bible to her on one of her birthdays, and she felt it was mostly needed today.

# Chapter 26

Katherine was in the hallway for Fr. Ryan to finish with the confessionals. She started thinking back when she just started coming here. Light was filtering through the stained glass windows high atop the chapel, casting light on the Bible sitting on the stand at the altar. It was a warm sign of hope Katherine had to focus on. She sat so still. She stood quietly waiting.

Jonathan had left her at the house only after she insisted. She had things to do, and talking to Fr. Ryan was one of them. Katherine was depressed and confused but didn't want to let Jonathan know. She had to count on Jonathan for support but needed Fr. Ryan for advice. She knew that his spiritual guidance would help her. Katherine kept remembering that the doctors wanted her to abort her baby. "Not this baby. Not my baby! We made her out of our love, and we'll bring her into this world with God's love. Whatever he decides. It will be his will and not mine or anybody else's."

At the other end of the rectory, Katherine could hear some conversation. Fr. Ryan was sending someone in the opposite direction from where they were now walking. Katherine could feel the nerves tingling down her back.

"Fr. Ryan," Katherine said, trying to be calm. "I was hoping that you would had a few minutes. I know that you're very busy, but I need to talk to you." With that, Katherine went into complete hysteria, cradling herself with trembling hands. Fr. Ryan was shocked.

He didn't expect it from her. He knew her for a few years, and she seemed so together.

"Katherine, well, of course I can talk to you. I can't imagine what's troubling you. Come into my office, and we'll talk right now." With that, Katherine gathered herself up and followed him into his office. She made herself comfortable in the chair while Fr. Ryan put some water in the kettle for hot tea.

Fr. Ryan listened, trying to console her. He understood her problems. He knew that what she was doing was right and God would watch over them. He closed the door so their conversation was between them and God.

She was so relieved to be there. Katherine found such peace within the confines of these walls. She wished that she could stay there forever.

# Chapter 27

The chapel was just as warm as Samantha remembered. The last time she was there, it was for Grandfather Henry's funeral. People sent wreaths of flowers from all over the world. The mourners numbered so many that there weren't enough seats. Many just stood in the back.

Samantha's mind wondered about her grandfather. She had heard rumors of his business dealings and ruthlessness but never wanted to believe them. She often heard her mother and father argue about how he was always interfering into their business. Grandfather was always trying to rule their home life. Her father, Marcus, wanted to move into their own house, but Grandfather wouldn't hear of it. Samantha got the opportunity to listen sometimes from behind locked doors. She never understood what was being said. She was always in fear of being caught, so, she would run off the minute any noise was uttered throughout the house.

Samantha started thinking about her mother giving up a child and moving to an unknown place. The hardships she must have felt not knowing anybody. Which child would stay and which one would go. How could this have happened? She was feeling quite motionless, listening to her own rhythm of breathing, when she noticed a few people in the church. As each began to leave, they went over to the candles in front of the pews and lit some. They placed their beads in their hands twisting as the Hail Marys were said. "Do I remember mine?" Samantha questioned herself.

Samantha walked up to the lined candles, some burning and others not. She knelt down in front of them, placing her Bible on the right ledge. She lit three candles: one for her mother, one for her sister, and one for herself. What seemed only a few minutes later, she felt another person next to her kneeling. So with closed eyes, she made sure that her prayers were done in silence, not to disturb this person.

The other person then got up and turned to Fr. Ryan, who was now standing in the doorway to his office and waved goodbye. When this woman was halfway down the aisle, Samantha opened her eyes and yelled out to this woman to stop. She noticed that she had taken her Bible by mistake. One was still sitting on the front pew.

"Wait, you've forgotten your Bible," repeated Samantha.

"No, I didn't, I have mine right here, see?"

They both stood two feet from each other displaying their Bibles.

And with that, Katherine produced her Bible from under her arm. It did look a little different. She thought hers was frayed more around the sides but the crest on the front of the covers were the same. Fr. Ryan came over to both women out of curiosity.

"I'm afraid that you have taken my Bible that was given to me on one of my birthdays, March 21, by my parents," said Samantha. Samantha had no idea why she was telling this total stranger this information.

"That's OK. I know mine by the inscription on the inside cover left to me after my mother died," Katherine continued. "With this book, you will find your way. Signed, Henry." She was pointing to the words in the Bible so Samantha could see.

Samantha opened the other Bible so Katherine could read it out loud. "With this book, you will find your way. Signed, Henry." Samantha's body and mind went numb. Her face was transfixed on Katherine as she fainted.

# Chapter 28

There were too many files Phillips had to go over. He hated flying and was exhausted from all the hassles that went along with his type of work. He had paid plenty for the right information, and he didn't want to leave any room for mistakes.

Phillips had his investigators talk to the office manager's son of years ago. He told them about some abandoned warehouse filled with files stacked up to the ceiling collecting years of dirt. Marcus didn't know what to do with them after Henry Von Burger's death. There was no love lost. Burying the cartons was like burying Henry Von Burger again. Beatrice didn't really want her father's business, so Marcus Rudolph watched over it from a very long distance. Marcus got quite used to the lifestyle his father-in-law provided. He didn't do much of anything over the years of their marriage. The birth of his daughter set an already-estranged marriage to the foreground. Neither spouse hardly talked to each other, and as the years went on, Marcus almost relied on their silence to get him through the years of his infidelity.

Phillips was in the warehouse with two of his buddies going over every scrap of paper. Business dealings with India's prime minister and other leaders from around the world arguing for better tariffs or no tariffs. Personnel files of all the workers, families, where they came from, and some not-so-legal ones. Nothing on Mary Donahue. It was going to take days to get through this mess. He had to find the whereabouts of Mary Donahue, mother of Samantha Rudolph Arpel.

If he calculated properly, she should be about sixty-five years of age, if she lived that long. His people were already looking up the obituaries as far back as they could. His only hope was that she stayed in these parts. Records were never opened to the public except when money crossed their palms.

"I've got to take a break from this awful dust. Come have a cigarette. We'll continue later after lunch," Phillips said, patting his head with a wet handkerchief.

"Wait a minute!" yelled his assistant, Paul. "Come here and look at this."

The file was under a dried-up piece of black leather that covered the writing area of the desk. It was cut in the lower corner, telling Phillips that it was obviously a hiding place. The rolltop desk had a tarnished gold plate bearing the name of Henry Von Burger across the top. Boxes were piled atop this poor antique. The rolltop was stuck in the halfway position, but one could see letters still in their original cubicles as if it were put there yesterday. Phillips took one out, and the envelope was dated December 12, 1940. He replaced it.

In his left hand was the file taken from underneath the leather. Because there were so much dust particles floating in the air, he had to get out. He did find the door and then went out rubbing his eyes, hoping that they would adjust quickly to the bright light.

"I'm dying for a drink. Could you get some water? Anything?" Mr. Phillips went through the file. He found an agreement setting up the marriage of their daughter Beatrice with Marcus Rudolph. All the arrangements were made and dowries listed all their assets from both parties and bank accounts. Birth certificates of both principals were enclosed.

"Here, Mr. Phillips, I found a cherry tonic for you." He then came to the most interesting piece of information. He never expected it. On the last page of this file, there was a picture of a funeral gathering. Mr. Phillips started reading the names in the group. Mr. Marcus Rudolph, at the age of thirteen, was at the funeral of his parents.

Next to this child was a young man, just a little older than Marcus, standing with his arms around him.

Mr. Phillips's heart began to beat faster. Not believing his eyes, he removed his glasses and squinted in the bright sunlight. There was absolutely no mistake. This other person next to Marcus was the person who married Beatrice Von Burger. Phillips dropped his handkerchief. "Oh my god, this can't be true!" This information was priceless, and he knew it.

# Chapter 29

Samantha was lying stretched out on the bench when she opened her eyes. She was now staring up at the Virgin Mother. Samantha was trying to recall what just happened but was interrupted when Fr. Ryan and Katherine came to her with a glass of water. Fr. Ryan was ready to call for medical help, but Samantha waved that idea off. Samantha sat up with the glass in her hands, so she put it down next to her. She stared at Katherine, looking for some shred of evidence to confirm her belief.

"Is this really happening?" she said to Fr. Ryan while studying Katherine. Samantha gathered herself into a sitting position and looked at Katherine. Samantha thought, "We don't look anything alike. She's beautiful. How can she be my sister, and to find her just at the beginning of my search? I don't understand any of this." Samantha studied Katherine's face, showing no signs of recognition.

"Are you all right?" asked Katherine.

Then Samantha caught a resemblance in the eyes. Sure enough, they were her father's. They were her father's eyes as sure as she was sitting there. Samantha was going to take a chance simply on a hunch. This was going to be a long shot, but she had to ask.

"You are not going to believe me, but I believe that I have been looking for you." Katherine looked at this woman as if she was crazy. "If you tell me that your last name is Donahue, then I'll know that I'm right." Samantha had to go on without stopping or she was not going to get it all out. She went on. "Many years ago, my mother gave birth to twins, and then for reasons I can't go into now, she split us up. I believe that you and I are those twins. I just learned of this information recently. I just started looking for you with the use of a detective agency."

"My last name is Donahue, but I don't even look like you, and besides, I don't even come from here," shrugged Katherine. "This is crazy! I don't know you. How do you know my name?"

"I know. I know that you come from Iowa City, where your, our mother worked in a furniture factory owned by Sir Henry Von Burger, my grandfather." Katherine was shivering as Samantha spoke. "That Bible you have is a family heirloom, and there is only one way you got it. My, our grandfather gave it to our mother before she left here with you. Grandfather signed the inside cover in his own handwriting. Look, they are both exactly the same. The only way you came across it was Henry Von Burger, my grandfather, your grandfather, gave it to your mother. No one could ever get their hands on them. It would never leave our family unless it was given to your mother. You said that your grandmother gave it to you. Where did she get it?"

Katherine started thinking about the day she gave it to her. Katherine's eyes told the rest of the answer. She remembered now. Grandmother knew the truth and gave it to her for her to find her destiny.

"Grandma Nettie said that it would play an important part in my life someday. I now know what she meant. My birthday is also on March 21. The same as yours. My name is Katherine Donahue from Iowa City, born March 21, 1944. "I came to this part of the country because my mother always talked about the ocean. She traveled across it just to come here and start a new life. She later sent for her mother, Nettie. That would make her your grandmother too." Katherine took a breath and went on, "Why did my mother split us up? Who is my father? I don't even know your name. Who are you? Why is this happening to me now? I can't believe that this is real." Katherine began crying.

Samantha put her arms around her twin sister, Katherine, and whispered into her twin sister's ear, "I am Samantha Rudolph Arpel.

I believe that we are twin sisters separated at birth. I believe she did it so our mother could keep at least one of us. Our father kept the only child he was told was born. Mary was sent to Iowa City with you. Our grandfather, Henry Von Burger, planned the whole thing."

"I would suspect that Mary had to promise not to publicize the illegitimacy of his grandchildren. Knowing him, he probably did just that. You see, our mother worked for Marcus Rudolph as a house-keeper, and she got pregnant by him with us. The shame would have profound effect on their good name and the family's position in the community."

"I can't believe that this should be happening now when every day is so precious to me. How can I have a twin sister? This has to be true. How does she know so much about me? Mom never talked about much. I used to ask her and Grandma Nettie with all her crazy stories of past. I need time to digest all this."

When Katherine heard this woman's name, she thought, "Samantha Rudolph Arpel! Is God playing a joke on me?" Katherine was in shock hearing her name. She was thinking that she was having an affair with a man who turned out to be her sister's husband. This couldn't be. Was she really living this horror, or was someone playing a terrible trick? Katherine sat there trying to figure this whole mess out. "Why me? What happened years ago?" Katherine was just beginning to put the pieces of the puzzle together. Her mother never really told her any information about her birth. She always seemed alone and depressed. Katherine knew that this had to be true some-how. Katherine was caught off balance when Samantha started play-ing with her fingers. Her mother did that when she was worried. Her own gut feeling was telling her so. Her own reason for coming to church today. She had to talk to Fr. Ryan about the baby. Oh my god, the baby.

Katherine said, "I'm going to have a baby, and I had to talk to Fr. Ryan. That's why I'm here today."

Samantha was crying with joy and disbelief. At the same time, Katherine was feeling total disbelief and shock.

All these unanswered questions.

Fr. Ryan stood there witnessing the reunion of two sisters separated at birth. Now, they were both holding on to each other with open arms and each with their Bibles in their hands. As a matter of fact, it was in the hands that the truth be told. When they were holding each other, they both got a glimpse at each other's hands, and then they knew that they were twin sisters. They already started thinking as one. Fr. Ryan smiled looking up at the Virgin Mary crossing himself. "Miracles do happen," he whispered and left them alone.

# Chapter 30

Samantha was holding onto the only living person whom she could connect with. In her whole life, there wasn't anybody to be there for her to share her deepest and most concerning feelings. As a young girl, loneliness became a condition and a way of life. She took it with her to her fourth-floor bedroom while it accompanied her to school and afternoon walks in the gardens. So alone growing up. Her loneliness was probably the main reason why she married Jonathan. Companionship was what she needed, not a husband. Since romance was lacking from the very start, their intimacy couldn't sustain itself. Now that major problems had settled in, disaster for the future was inescapable.

Why did she have to be the only child? Having a brother or sister would have made her life more tolerable. The thought of having a sister was so strange to her. Too many years had gone by, and personal memories just blended into a blob of images hardly remembered. Why didn't Beatrice and her father ever tell her that Beatrice wasn't her real mother? How embarrassing for her, for them. They couldn't let this information out. What a scandal! Discredited the family name of the Von Burgers. Samantha's head was whirling questions, answers, thoughts, and forethoughts. She was answering her own questions and asking herself new ones, too.

Katherine was still trying to figure out being raised in Iowa City, poor as a church mouse with her mother and grandmother. Why didn't anybody from the family help them? There were lonely times for her. She didn't have friends of her own to talk to, and now she had a sister. Not just a sister, but a twin sister. What went on in those years? Arranged marriage? How barbaric!

Samantha was not about to let Katherine out of her sight. "Katherine, come over to my house. I have so many questions to ask you about our mother. Do I look anything like her? Was she a good mother, and did she hug you a lot? Beatrice never hugged me. Now I know why. You said that she died, how and when? What about our grandmother? What was her name, and what did she say again about the Bible we both have?" Samantha was terrified to lose her sister and was gobbling her up with questions.

"Actually, I don't feel too well, and I'd like to go home. This has been a shock to me, and I have to rest. There is so much going on here, and I've got to lie down. Would you care to come over to my home so we could talk?"

With both women in agreement, they left the church. Their arms were twisted together like old friends meeting for a shopping trip. They had a different bounce in their walk, and a hidden joy of love reached inside each for the other. Oh, yes, they were definitely sisters.

Fr. Ryan was so thrilled to help these two strangers realize the benevolence in returning to the church. Each one for their own reasons. Samantha and Katherine found something neither would or could believe at first. He believed that their destiny was planned. The day they were born and separated, was the day they would be together, no matter which road they traveled. Different views, different lifestyles, even different parts of the country. It didn't matter. They were supposed to be together someday because God wanted it that way.

*Chapter 31*

P hillips was too excited to wait for phone calls and timetables. He told Paul to continue looking for information that would help find Mary Donahue and made up some excuse to leave. He had to get back home. He kept the information out of the reach of Paul's eyes.

"Where are you going so fast? You just got here. Why are you leaving without finishing up our search for Mary Donahue?" asked a puzzled Paul. His whole face was in a distorted facial expression. One of an idiot, or was it the sun in his face that gave Mr. Phillips the sick feeling of why did he hire him in the first place?

"That's why I hired you, Paul. I knew that you could figure out the whereabouts of Mary. You'll let me know, right? If you find out any information, call me. You hear? The information in the folder was nothing but bills."

His mind was scattered all over the states, actually all over the world. Wow, he'd have to buy this. This was too much. He was going to pay top dollar for this. Phillips was seeing dollar signs. "I can retire for life with what I have in this folder. Who is this man who calls himself Marcus Rudolph? What a colossal find. I bet Sir Henry Von Burger knew this all along or pretty soon after the wedding. He was too clever to be fooled. What happened years ago?" Phillips couldn't sit in the airplane, so he was up a number of times to the bathroom. Phillips was seeing dollar signs everywhere. "I'll tell Samantha that

Paul is still researching and I had to come home. Not feeling too well. What did happen to the real Mr. Marcus Rudolph?"

Layers of deception were completely covering this family. This so-called family of the community. The truth was about to surface, and Phillips wanted to be there.

It was rather strange for Marcus to answer his own phone, except he was so close to it. Marcus hardly had the receiver next to his ear when he heard a voice asking for Mr. Marcus Rudolph. "Yes, this is Marcus Rudolph. What can I do for you?"

Beatrice was shouting, "Who is calling?" Marcus shrugged his shoulders.

"I asked for the real Mr. Marcus Rudolph. Do you know where he is?" with a short hesitation. "Is this Mr. Peterson? Do you understand what I am asking? Do I make myself clear with my questions, or do I have to explain?" Marcus began feeling sick to his stomach. "I'd rather talk to him, but since I can't, I guess I have to talk to you. Whoever you are tonight."

There were so many questions. In a way, Marcus was waiting for this day. He didn't know how Henry found out about his identity but promised not to embarrass the family at any cost. They had an ongoing hatred for each other that Beatrice couldn't understand. Something happened after the wedding, and Father wouldn't discuss it with her. Marcus never worked, and Henry never spoke to him. Beatrice didn't do anything. After all, she had a new husband, tall, handsome, maybe a little older than she thought, but she was happy.

"I don't know what you're talking about, but you better not call here again or I'll call the police." Marcus was firm in his tone, but only laughter came from the other end of the line.

"You think that a man like you could get away with murder and impersonation? I know that you are not who you say you are. I also know that Sir Henry Von Burger knew."

Marcus was about to hang up, but his hand was paralyzed and had to listen to everything. Someday he knew that his secret would come out. How or who would blow his cover, he didn't know. He just knew that someday it would happen.

"Meet me tonight at twelve at Journeymen's End at the end of Route 4." With that, there was silence on the line.

# Chapter 32

Katherine was making some tea as Samantha was wandering around her small home. It was beautiful with all the little antiques of blue and white, brass, and iron lanterns and walls covered with old pictures.

"Do you know any of these people in those pictures?" asked a very curious Samantha. Katherine started laughing and crying at the same time. Samantha didn't think that her question was going to upset her, so she asked who some of the people were. Katherine cleared her throat.

"Whenever I went rummaging through piles of junk at flea markets, I always asked about the people in the pictures. I can't believe you just asked me the same questions. No, I don't know anybody in any of those pictures. I just liked the frames." Both women could feel emotions drawing them closer.

Tea was made, and they sat across the kitchen table from each other and stared. The smell of the herbal tea had a calming effect on each. They started to relax with each other, yet, with guarded reactions to each other's questions. Each searching for some more proof of their sisterhood.

Samantha asked questions about Mary. "What kind of a mother she was and Grandma Nettie?" Samantha thought that coming from Ireland must have been awful with no money. Working as a housekeeper must have been so degrading. Samantha started to say something, and Katherine then finished her sentence. Both were in shock and started laughing. Samantha was feeling a little like a snob with her questions about poverty, and now she felt embarrassed about her feelings. Katherine knew and understood.

Katherine had to clear the air and mystery about her baby, but not yet. This was going to be tough. She found a sister she didn't even know that she had. She could understand why Jonathan fell in love with Samantha. She was the most likeable and congenial person she had ever met. "She made me feel so comfortable about my baby, and she didn't even ask me who the father is."

Katherine knew that she had to tell Samantha about the father of the baby, but she couldn't get it out. Katherine had to tell her the truth. She had to be told. She had to talk to Jonathan immediately.

"Before you had asked me about my baby and her father. Well, I'll get to that some other time. Right now, all I want is to get to know you. I can't believe that I have a sister." Katherine put her hand on Samantha's, and they both were so proud of each other. "Please tell me about my father, our father, Marcus Rudolph."

Samantha was sitting with all senses working.

"Our father left me alone a lot. He really didn't spend much time with me. Mother always made excuses why he wasn't around, and when he was, there was little contact with him. He was always too busy doing whatever he did. But I couldn't even figure out what he did. I guess I thought that he worked with our grandfather, Henry Von Burger, doing something with textiles or furniture, but I was never sure. I wasn't allowed to ask. I spend most of the time going to school and doing what was expected of me. When I went away to school, I fell head over heels for Jonathan, and we married without telling anybody. Boy, were they surprised. I've never done anything in my whole life without asking permission for something. Can you imagine, me running off and marrying somebody they didn't even meet?"

Katherine tried to pour herself cup of tea hoping that the mist of the mint tea would calm the pounding of her heart. She was trembling so much that she had to put the teacup down. Guilt was getting to her, and her heart was breaking. Sweat was pouring off her brow.

Katherine was beginning to feel quite sick to her stomach. She started thinking about what was really happening. Samantha was in the dark about the real condition of her sister. "You idiot. Who do you think you are? You're going to have Jonathan's baby, and here you sit with his wife, your sister. You fool. Thought that having an affair with Jonathan wasn't going to have its repercussions? Now look at what you've done! I have to talk to Jonathan."

"Katherine, are you all right?"

"I was told that I have a brain tumor that can't be operated on because of where it's located." Katherine blurted it out without stopping. "I was in church talking to Fr. Ryan about what I want to do. I needed his help to make some decisions, but I came to realize that it is totally up to me. You see, the tumor's treatment is with chemicals. I can't wait. I can't have treatment while I'll pregnant, and I wouldn't have an abortion. Do I have to say any more? These men doctors want me to abort and have treatment. I will not do that, and I will have this baby. Do you understand?" By now, Katherine was in tears, and no tea in the world could help her now.

Samantha wrapped her arms around her. There was such comfort in helping her. Being there for her. "This new person called my sister, called Katherine Donahue." Tears were rolling down both their faces. Samantha knew that she was going to be there for her sister. Katherine was going to have this child.

"Katherine, God brought us together in his own crazy way, and he will help us through this. I have to believe that. You keep your baby, and God will watch over you and her. He's not going to allow anything bad to happen to either of you. Don't you understand? He brought you and me together from millions of places that you could have lived. You picked here to live, and we found each other." Samantha paused.

By now, Katherine was sobbing uncontrollably. Samantha was getting very worried if her condition got any worse. "Katherine, please calm yourself." Samantha was rocking her in her arms like a baby.

"You don't understand, Samantha, there is more, and I have to tell you."

Samantha's mind couldn't possibly consider what else. Streams of tears flowed down her face, nose running, sobbing.

"Please, I beg of you, please don't hate me. I didn't know."

Samantha sat there shocked. What was she saying? She didn't understand why all this pleading.

"Please, Samantha, we just found each other, and I don't want to lose you. You are my twin sister, my own flesh and blood, and I don't know how this happened." Katherine took a deep breath. "We just didn't share the same mother and father." Samantha was sitting there waiting for each word to come out of her mouth. She was not understanding anything she was saying. "Jonathan is the father of my baby. Your husband, Jonathan Arpel, and I have been having an affair, and now I am pregnant with his baby, your husband. Please don't hate me. I didn't know. Please?" Katherine was pleading.

Samantha was sitting there in her twin sister's kitchen. Now she understood all the crying. Now she understood all the days and nights alone. Now she understood. He was having an affair with Katherine. Katherine just happened to be her twin sister. "I can't believe this. Nobody would believe it. A baby with her. Why not with me, his wife?" Samantha was just sitting there very calmly trying to take this all in. Katherine stopped crying and was waiting for some reaction from Samantha.

"Please say something, Samantha. Please don't hate me. I beg you, please don't hate me. Please don't hate Jonathan."

# Chapter 33

It was later than Marcus thought. He had to get out of the house. He told Beatrice that he had a dinner with some men. He said that he might be home very late. Don't wait up for him. What did this man know? It had been so many years. Why would this be happening to him now? Where did I know his voice from? How much would he want to keep his mouth shut? Marcus was about to learn all the answers soon. Was his charade coming to a close? Not if he could help it. Nothing was going to ruin his life.

Phillips was not able to reach Samantha. He really didn't want to talk to her. He didn't want her to know that he was back in town. He would call back tomorrow and pretend he was calling from Iowa.

He made all the copies of the picture and placed them carefully in different envelopes. He then sealed them and placed them all in his car trunk ready for mailing tomorrow. He left the original in the front seat and set off to meet Mr. Marcus Rudolph. "Or whoever or whatever you call yourself," he thought. "How much money should I tell him? I know, I tell him all the copies are in the mail to people of prominence, and if I die, they will all be notified. I can't wait to see the look on his face. Wow, is he going to be shocked. All these years of lying. Oh, man, he's really going to pay for this, and I'm going on vacation. A very long vacation for the rest of my life. I don't care about what happens to Samantha. He's paying. He's paying through the nose, whoever he is."

The road up to Journeyman's End was more treacherous than Marcus ever expected. Fog set in, and the windows kept getting all cloudy. Phillips got up to Journeyman's End, except Marcus was there first. He got out of the car and had to hold on. The roads up there were all rocky, and the handle to the car door felt good in his right hand.

"Who's there?" asked Marcus, barely able to see a shadow. The air was so thick, and he couldn't see anything except the outline of a man walking closer as he approached from the car. The car lights were on, and that made seeing more difficult.

Oh, but Phillips could see Marcus just fine. "Hello there. Do you know who I am?" Marcus then recognized the figure coming up to him. He remembered doing some work for him in the past. "What did he want, and what am I doing up here?" Questioning himself, he blurted out, "What the hell do you want from me? You said that you have some information to bring a scandal to my family, and I don't know what you are talking about."

"Oh, yes, you do. I know that you are not the real Marcus Rudolph, but I do believe that you did know him. From the old country. I don't know how all this happened, but you are not him." Phillips took out the picture of the funeral with a group of people standing around the cemetery. "See, you're not in the right place. Look, that's you. You married Beatrice Von Burger under false pretense, and I know that Henry knew, didn't he? Who are you?"

Frustrated by all this incomplete information, Phillips was now so close to Marcus that their noses were almost touching. Their breaths was getting mixed up with each other's, climaxing into a steady stream of moisture pouring in the direction that only the wind decided where to take it. Marcus grabbed Phillips arm and bent it back. The footing at the ledge of the canyon was untrustworthy. Rocks started to move under their feet. Phillips didn't stop talking about his information, and Marcus belted him in the right side of his face.

"Shut up, you idiot." Marcus was sitting on top of Phillip's chest. "I saw the real Marcus Rudolph go overboard in a storm, and

I won't stop at anything to keep my secret just that, a secret. What do you want?"

"Money, what else?"

"How much?"

"Three million dollars."

Marcus got so enraged that his mind went out of control. He pulled Phillips up to a standing position and smacked him in the right shoulder. Phillips started to duck. He remembered that when you couldn't fight him, duck and run. Marcus came after him with another swing, and Phillips ducked again. This time Marcus lost his footing. Phillips realized what was happening and tried to reach out.

He wanted to blackmail him. He didn't want him dead. That was the last thing he wanted. He was going to be his meal ticket for life. Their fingers grazed each other's, but their gloves wouldn't connect. Marcus, in grabbing for Phillip's hand, ripped the photo out of Phillip's grip, and before his very eyes, Marcus Rudolph was over the edge of the canyon. Nothing was left but the empty air of the blackened mist. Fog wiped out anything that had just happened and left no traces of humankind. The silence was deafening. The cold air blowing across his face was piercing his ears and soon brought him back to reality.

Phillips was so shaken up that he had to sit there. What would he tell the police? Why was he up here with him? "Samantha is going to learn of her father's death. Should I speak up? No, you idiot, keep your mouth shut." He had to get up now and start cleaning his overcoat. Dirt was covering his entire coat and inside his sleeves. He could smell death nearby, and he had to leave. Panic was forcing his legs to stumble through the darkened path, which led him back to his car. He found himself talking to himself in disbelief. "This son of a bitch had to die. He was going to take care of everything for me." Phillips felt a stinging pain from his arm, and when he looked down briefly, he could see some blood oozing from his wrist. He must have brushed up against some branches when he was running back to the car. As he was leaning against the car, he was trying to recall all that was said.

"Did he say that he saw Marcus go overboard on a ship?" His mind was trying to recall everything he said.

"Oh my god, I'm getting the hell out of here."

Phillips got in the car and drove wildly down the twisted canyon road. His mind was trying to sort out things. "Maybe I could get money from his family? Then they would think I killed him. I better stay quiet for a while." He then started to slow down so no one would take notice. Take notice, there wasn't anyone. "Who would be so crazy to be up here in this cold chilling fog anyways?" he thought. "How ironic. I just saw one Marcus Rudolph fall over the ledge of Journeymen's End, and that Marcus Rudolph witnessed the real one go to his death overboard. How ironic?"

Phillip's mind was now back to being an investigator. Now, the police. The investigation. No one saw him. He was clear, or was he? Should he call the police? After all, he was the detective just asking Marcus some questions when he went crazy and started to fight with him. Why was he up the hill in the middle of the night? Why not question him at his house? After all, these questions would have to be resolved before he called any police. He decided to go back to his office to check messages, and there weren't any.

# Chapter 34

Jonathan was frantic with worry. He called Katherine all day and got a busy signal. He knew that she took the receiver off the phone when she rested. She did take the phone off the hook, but she wasn't resting. He placed a call to home and got no answer. He didn't want to go home, and he wasn't going over to Katherine's if she was sleeping. For some reason, he felt very alone. He felt so helpless.

Katherine and Samantha decided that it would be best if each were to get some sleep. It was time for Samantha to go home and let all that has happened sink in. She was in shock now knowing about her husband, now knowing about her sister. Brain tumors, babies, affairs, husband, sister, mother, no mother. Samantha and Katherine agreed that they both would talk to Jonathan. He was going to be in shock that all this was out in the open. Katherine laid down on the sofa with another gift from her mother. A hand-knitted afghan that Mary made and believed would take all the pain and doubts away.

Samantha went to bed as soon as she got home. Visions, images were floating around in her head. Remembering everything her sister told her today. Was it just one day? She didn't even know if she was mad at Jonathan or just relieved that she knew her instincts were right. Her mother did tell her that every woman knew her own husband. She would never ever doubt her instincts. She was too exhausted to think anymore. "I can't think anymore." She did have to make future plans but couldn't possibly begin to comprehend what was about to become public.

"It's time to talk to my father and set some things straight with him. Just imagine. He doesn't even know that another child was born, a twin. No more questions, no more answers, no more deception, just sleep. Please. I'm glad Katherine told me about Jonathan. I just want to sleep now."

# Chapter 35

The phone was ringing in Jonathan's office, and he knocked himself on the desk trying to reach it on the fourth ring.

"Hello?"

"Darling, it's me."

"Katherine, are you all right?" Jonathan was trying to keep his frustration to a minimum.

"I have had the most incredible day, Jonathan. You won't believe it. We have so much to talk about. Can you come over now? I met someone today. Jonathan, you won't believe who it is. Jonathan, are you still there? Say something."

"Who did you meet? I can't imagine who you met. Please tell me."

"Jonathan, I can't tell you until you come over. Please hurry. I'll be waiting."

Katherine was scared and frustrated at the same time. "How is Jonathan going to react after learning that I met Samantha? How is he going to comprehend that we are sisters, twin sisters?" Katherine was beginning to feel that Jonathan wasn't going to understand why she had to tell Samantha. "He is going to go out of his mind. What if he gets upset with me?" By now, Katherine was talking to herself out loud. "Now I'm pregnant, and the doctors tell me that I have a tumor. They're crazy. I feel fine. No medication. No treatment till I have this baby. Oh, where is Jonathan? He's not going to believe this.

How am I going to prepare him for this? He will go crazy." Katherine was pacing the floors, talking to herself. "I have a sister now. She's wonderful. I love her. How can I? I am having a baby with her husband. This is ridiculous. Oh my god, where's Jonathan?"

Upon hearing the car door slam, Katherine raced to open the front door. She then realized how exhausted she really was. She thought, "Is she going to make it through this with Jonathan? Oh, please help me," and crossed herself. She opened the door, and a frantic Jonathan came through with gaping hugs and kisses.

"Katherine, what's going on? Have you found some encouraging news about the treatment for the tumor? What? Tell me now. The baby?" He was completely frustrated by her actions and the big mystery.

"Sit down and I'll make a drink." Katherine was very resourceful in managing him now. He would have stood on his head just to get it out of her. He behaved exactly according to direction, and now all was set. Katherine had to continue. No more delays.

Katherine was on her feet rubbing her hand together mustering up the guts. She didn't know where to start, so she decided to start at the beginning, at church.

"Jonathan, sometimes things happen and we don't know exactly why at the time," she started. "So many things have happened in my life. Meeting you and now the baby. Where I lived and grew up. My mother dying and then moving here. I didn't know why I desired to move here, I just did. I met you and fell in love with a wonderful man who happens to be married. I didn't want to, but I did." With that pause, Katherine sat down next to Jonathan hoping that what she was about to do wouldn't destroy everything they have together. Change, yes, but not destroy. Only their love would hold them together now.

Katherine took Jonathan's hand on her lap and placed the family Bible in it. Jonathan looked quite puzzled for a moment and then saw the crest on the outer cover. His hands were holding it, and when he realized what it saw, he let it go as if it were on fire.

"Katherine, what are you doing with this Bible? It belongs to Samantha's family. I have seen this Bible for years, and I know it well.

Why do you have it?" Jonathan was totally rattled and on his feet pacing waiting for an answer.

"Here it goes," she thought.

"Something happened in church today that is going to change my life forever. I met a woman with the same Bible that I had. We went there for different reasons but came to the same conclusions. We talked, and I found out that many years ago, a set of twin girls were born and then separated. Each to find their way to each other many years later, and that has happened to me today. In church. She placed her Bible next to mine. I then got up to go, and she thought I took her book. It turned out that both Bibles were given to us under different circumstances but by the same person. Our grandfather, Mr. Henry Von Burger. Through conversation, I learned that she had been looking for me since she just recently learned of this information. Jonathan, I have a twin sister. She doesn't even look like me. We have the same birthday, and she had information all about my mother. She thought that her mother was the woman that brought her up. Oh, it's all so confusing. Many years ago, her father had had an affair with the housekeeper, our real mother, my mother. Oh, don't you see? I have a sister!

"Inside each Bible was written the same inscription, and Jonathan, you must know by now who I am talking about. Look inside. See here, 'With this book, you shall find your way. Signed, Henry.' Jonathan, it's Samantha. It was given to her by Henry Von Burger, her grandfather, and he must have given my mother the same book before he helped her relocate to Iowa City, where I grew up. She worked in his factory. All the pieces fit. Except, we didn't know that you and I would fall in love. Jonathan, say something. Please say something."

Shock took over his body, and numbness froze his limbs. All he could think of was, that his wife, Samantha, found out about them. How hurt she must be. "I am such a fool. How could all this happen to me?" The last thing in the world was to hurt Samantha. "Oh, my poor wife, Samantha. What a mess. What a fool I was to think I could get away with this." Feeling was coming back to his legs, and he could move again. Pulling himself up from the couch, he felt like he was going to throw up. Shame and hate for himself. Hate for Katherine.

"Katherine, you told her about us and then about the baby? You actually told her that we were going to have this baby and it could kill you having it? Are you crazy? Telling her that we were having an affair wasn't right. How could you do this to me without telling me first what was happening? How could you?" Jonathan was turning green.

Trembling with nausea, he had to pour another drink to calm his shaking hands. He was now trapped into something he didn't want. "How could she do this to me without talking to me first?" Jonathan was absolutely furious with her. He was heading for the door.

"Where are you going? Jonathan, I thought that you would understand what went on today. I found my sister. My twin sister that I didn't know that I had. I must find out the truth about my life. We plan on meeting tomorrow. Please try to understand. Samantha is going to understand about us. I had to tell her." She just about caught her breath. "Where are you going?" she was yelling.

He was out the door.

# Chapter 36

Beatrice was getting very worried when Marcus didn't come home, and it was already three in the morning. He had been late on occasion, but never this late. She wandered the whole house never realizing how big it really was especially now that it was so void of family. So quiet. Only the years of memories.

A long list of familiar faces that graced these walls and gala affairs. Parties given for the new governor of Massachusetts was held here. Beatrice was trying to remember the last time the house was filled with festivities when her thoughts were interrupted by knocking on the front door.

"My lord, who in the world would be at my door at this hour?" she said. "Marcus probably forgot his keys or he had too much to drink. Wait a minute, who's there?"

"Police, Mrs. Rudolph. Please let us in."

"What in the world would they be coming out here?" she thought, opening the door. She could tell that something was wrong. The two officers had their hats in their hands and didn't even ask to come in. They just came into the foyer and closed the door. The cold night air gripped Beatrice by the throat, and she wrapped the collar of her robe closer to her neck while leading the officers into the living room.

"What's the meaning of this intrusion? Gentlemen?" She then directed them to the two sofas in the middle of the living room.

"I think that you, Mrs. Rudolph, should sit down. We're here to tell you that Mr. Rudolph has had an accident, and we want you to come to the hospital. We don't know what exactly happened except he is there." Officer Jenkins bowed his head and indicated that things didn't look good for Marcus.

"What kind of accident do you mean? A car accident?" She was shocked.

"Mrs. Rudolph, we are wasting time. Please get dressed now and come with us. We can talk later."

Beatrice was on her way to the hospital with these two strangers in a police car. She should have called Samantha or Jonathan to meet her there. What happened? What could have happened at a meeting with some men? Where was the meeting? She didn't remember what Marcus said to her. Why couldn't she remember what he said? She was trying to retrace her conversation with him earlier.

The police car stopped at the emergency entrance, and Beatrice was greeted by the chief of staff and two other gentlemen. A gust of frigid air blew across her face, slapping her into reality. Beatrice was helped into the hospital by the two policemen. "Beatrice, I am so sorry. Marcus has had an accident, and he's gone. He was found when two police officers spotted his car up there. He was up in the hills of Journeymen's End, and it seemed that he fell over the cliff. What was he doing up there in the first place? His car was parked about twenty feet away from the ledge. Did he have any problems with the car?"

Beatrice only heard that he was gone and had no idea when her legs went forward and she remembered grabbing an arm.

"Oh shit, she's fainted. Bring her into the waiting room. That's no way to break the news to a lady like this. She's too fragile."

They wheeled her into a private waiting room and placed her on the sofa. A nurse ran to get the smelling salt and water while another retrieved a pillow from the nearest closet for her head.

The chief of staff of the hospital was bending over her when Beatrice opened her eyes. Beatrice realized what was said and grabbed hold of the doctor's shoulder.

"Are you telling me that my husband is dead?"

"Yes, Mrs. Rudolph. I'm so very sorry. Marcus is gone. Can I call your daughter, Samantha, and Jonathan?

"What do you mean he's dead? All he did was to go to a meeting, and now you tell me that my husband is dead? I don't understand. How did he die? Did he have a heart attack? Did he have a car accident?"

"We don't really know except he fell over the ledge of Journeymen's End. Police found his car parked up there and, while looking for a passenger in the car, looked over the canyon, and there he was. Please, let me call someone."

Beatrice grew very angry with so little information about her husband. "I want to talk to the police again."

She sat up and fixed herself for what one would think as company arriving for dinner. She straightened her dress, feathered her fingers through her hair, and then put lipstick on. The room was rather dark, and she asked if she could use the bathroom. With an affirmative answer from the chief of staff, she entered the bathroom only to see a stranger looking at her from the mirror in front of her. "Who is the woman I'm staring at? She looks so old. This can't be me. I don't look like this." Her mind flashed back to her younger days of dating Marcus and their courtship.

He was very attentive when they first met even though it was under such awkward circumstances. His broken leg and all those bandages. He did take her by surprise, and he turned out to be more manly than she expected. She was so young in those days and waiting for a young boy coming off the ship. Instead there sat this full-grown man. After getting to know him, she liked his overbearing, yet, genteel personality. He was always excessively polite, which she felt came from his well-bred family history. It was quite thrilling to be in his arms and to learn from him what it's like to be a full-grown woman. Oh, yes, she fell for Mr. Marcus Rudolph.

The six-month courtship followed, and they were married with all the best that money could buy. All the right people were there as witness to this historic event. The best of Boston. A wedding that would be the talk of the town for months. "The perfect couple" was what the *Boston Globe* quoted in the society columns. "Daughter of Sir Henry Von Burger weds Mr. Marcus Rudolph" headlines everywhere.

Beatrice inwardly smiled at her reflection looking back at herself. If only they knew. She didn't know what went wrong after a year or two, but her husband wasn't coming home at night, and there were rumors of other women. She ignored them, and then the baby. "Oh, Mary's baby. How could I have gone along with such deceit for so long? Poor Samantha. I should have told her years ago. I did love her, but she wasn't mine, and I am sure that she felt something wrong. I didn't mean to be so cold. I just couldn't warm up to this child that was not mine." Beatrice started questioning herself. "Do I want to call her now and ruin her night's sleep? No, of course not. Marcus and I have ruined her life with lies and untruths. Now, she cannot seek the truth from him since he is no longer here. She will have to live with it. Samantha can learn of her father's death in the morning. I'll call her first thing. Marcus Rudolph is now dead, and I am all alone."

She was then interrupted by the knocking coming from outside the bathroom door. A detective was introducing himself. "Mrs. Rudolph, I am Detective Michael O'Shea. I'm so sorry to learn about your husband. I am with the Boston Police Department. I would like to talk to you." He was leading her into the other room where they could sit down. She noticed two more police officers near.

"Mrs. Rudolph, do have any ideas why your husband was up in the canyon? Did he discuss meeting anyone before he went out last night?" His questions were very disturbing to her, but all she did was shake her head back and forth indicating no. Words couldn't come out of her mouth.

"Mrs. Rudolph, I am going to show you something, a picture. We found it in your husband's hand rolled up as if he was up there with someone. Would you be so kind as to look at it and tell me if you recognize anybody in it?" He motioned to the other officers to bring the lamp closer so Mrs. Rudolph wouldn't have to move out of her seat. She leaned over. She gazed down at the old torn picture of a group of people. It seemed to be someone's funeral. "That's right," she thought. It was all a blur of a newspaper clipping of someone's funeral with people standing around, and names were at the bottom. "I can't see the names and hardly see the faces. I need my glasses."

"We would appreciate it if you put your glasses on, but we will cover up the names so you can properly identify the people in the photo." She thought that very strange but obliged.

It was very late, and Beatrice was exhausted. She positioned her glasses on her nose and studied the photo.

There were people standing around the gravesite of someone, and in the first row of mourners, she recognized Marcus standing with his arms resting on the shoulders of a younger and shorter boy. It was definitely Marcus.

"Here," she said, pointing to Marcus's face. "There. There's Marcus at somebody's funeral. He's fourth from the end. Yes, that's him. Whose is it, the funeral, that is? Why are you questioning me about a funeral, and why is Marcus—" Beatrice was interrupted.

"Now, Beatrice, please read all the names listed at the bottom of the photo. Read them very carefully so there are no mistakes."

"Oh my god, who is this man?" Beatrice was studying the photo, and a rush of heat went through her body. "What is the meaning of this picture? I want some answers. Who is this man?" Beatrice was now shouting. She was up out of the chair and quite different than just a couple of minutes ago. The police officers saw a transformation from a gentle lady to a mad woman. She could feel her heart racing and its beating becoming faster as the seconds past.

She only wanted to go back to the mirror. Where was that mirror? The mirror with all the answers. Go back to the past and find out what was going on here. "Who was this man? My father must have had something to do with this. Nothing got past him. Where did this photo come from?"

The picture told the answer, but she could not believe her eyes. What was the meaning of this? Beatrice sat down and placed the photo in her lap. Studying every detail, she knew something wasn't right. Too many years of hate between her father and her husband. Something was wrong, and never a word was mentioned as to why. Where did all their dreams go after the first year of their marriage?

"I was supposed to live happily ever after," she whispered. "My father told me so. What a joke! He should only know what has happened to me now. I don't even know the man I was married to, but I would bet everything that my father did. What did I do to deserve this? Oh my god, I don't even know who I am."

Beatrice sat in a strange room somewhere in a hospital feeling quite alone. Feelings of contempt came over her, and the death of her husband took second to her own feelings. Who was she? What were the next steps to follow?

# Chapter 37

M orning came too soon for Phillips when he twisted out of bed still deciding what to do about last night. The air was cold when he went to get the newspaper outside the door. A simple reminder of last night's event. How could he explain his presence with Marcus Rudolph to the police? He had been in some compromising situations before, but never like this one. Maybe the police wouldn't even ask him questions. "I could tell them I was there to discuss information about Samantha and the fact that she knew about who was her real mother. That's it. I'll tell them that I was investigating Samantha's mother and wanted to talk to Marcus alone even though Samantha told me not to speak to him. No, I'll say nothing to anybody."

"Oh, darn, who's calling now?" he mumbled.

"I expected to hear from you before I had to call you. You won't believe what I've found since you went to Iowa. In a way, Iowa came here." Samantha didn't have time to even ask him what he had found. She didn't know that he came back.

Samantha talked on about all that had happened since they last spoke. Repeating it all solidified the wonderful feelings of the day. She found her sister out of millions of places and people. Phillips sat listening dumbfounded. As she was going on about her sister, his mind was deep in thought about her father. He couldn't say anything. "Keep your mouth shut," he warned himself.

"Samantha, that's incredible."

"I spoke to your assistant, Paul. He called here looking for you this morning, and he told me that you found some photo. He didn't know what was in it. Did it have something to do with my sister and mother?"

"What I found had nothing to do with anything, and Paul shouldn't have even mentioned it since it had nothing to do with anything." Phillips was furious. The mere mention of a photo would put him in jeopardy. The sweat was now pouring off his forehead and the back of his neck. Why did Paul mention the photo? Where was the cold air now? He felt sick to his stomach.

"What do you want me to do now that you have found your sister and information about your mother? You now know about your husband and what he's been doing. I can't believe she told you, but I will never underestimate the power of blood in the family. I guess we can call this case closed."

"If I need you any further, I'll call you, and thank you for all you've done. Send me a bill, and remember, please don't talk to anybody about this. I want to confront him myself with my sister. What I do with my marriage is something that I have to decide later. There's lots to resolve first. Thanks."

Phillips was listening to the empty end of the line. "She doesn't know yet. The police or anybody hasn't found the body yet. I guess the world doesn't know what happened to Marcus Rudolph. I can relax. I'm fine."

# Chapter 38

Samantha couldn't get over sleeping through the entire night. So much happened yesterday. Jonathan didn't come home, so she could get dressed without confronting him. She didn't really know how she felt about him. Telling Phillips was wonderful. She and her sister were going to confront their father today and produce some intriguing information that would even make a good book. Samantha showered, cleaned up the bedroom, and was grabbing the keys to the car when the phone rang.

"I'll never get out of here. I wonder if it's Katherine. Hello?"

"Hello, my darling Samantha, it's Mother Beatrice." Samantha knew something was strange. She never called her my darling.

"Mom, you won't believe what I found yesterday. I want to come over and talk to you and Father today. I have someone I want you to meet." Samantha was about to go on but was sternly interrupted.

"Samantha, I have something upsetting to tell you. I don't want you to hear it from reporters or on the news. Samantha, darling, your father passed away last night."

Sam was trying to comprehend what was just said. "This can't be right. We were going over to confront our father and get to the bottom of this lie."

"There are so many unanswered right now. Please come over and don't answer any questions from anyone. I'm so sorry. I had to tell you this, but I need you right now. Please come over."

Samantha put the receiver down, sitting very still so as not to disturb this moment. Her father was dead. How? She was going to introduce his other daughter to him. Would he have cared? Beatrice must meet her. Meet her now. She picked up her keys and ran out the door without calling Katherine about their father. She wanted to tell her herself.

Katherine was waiting outside of the house. It was about 11:00 a.m. when Samantha arrived and Katherine jumped in and buckled up. "Let's go. How do I look? Do you think he'll like me? I'm so nervous about meeting the man I thought about so often. You know, what did he look like and what would he be? You know? Excuse me, why are you driving so fast?"

Tears started to pour down Samantha's face, and a look of horror reflected Katherine's. "What's wrong?"

"I just got a call from my mother, and she said that Marcus died. I must get over there. I can't believe it. I wanted you to meet your father and ask him all of the right questions so we could get on with our lives. I believe that he didn't know that you existed. Now he's gone, and Mother didn't say how he died except to get over." Samantha continued driving while wiping her sleeve over her cheeks since it was all she had with her. "I didn't have a chance to tell mother about you. It all was said so fast. You must meet her. She'll need us now. Oh, what a mess! Why is all this happening?"

Katherine felt such betrayal, and Samantha could feel it. She forgot all about herself and reached over to her sister Katherine's, arm, who was in such deep thought. "Don't worry, I'll always be there for you." Now Katherine was crying for a man whom she had never met but was about to. Marcus, her real father, now for some reason God decided to take him from her. They sat in silence until the mass of reporters surrounded Samantha's car as she slowed down to enter the front gate. They were both in shock.

Samantha pushed her way through them and grabbed Katherine's elbow, leading her first. She didn't want anybody to hurt her sister. They entered the foyer trying to avoid a collision of family lawyers, close friends, and doctors.

"Oh, Samantha, Jonathan is coming right over from the office. We called him the minute Beatrice called us. What a terrible accident!" someone said from the foyer. Samantha still didn't know what happened. She raced past all the familiar belongings to her mother. Beatrice was sitting on the sofa with Mrs. Webster.

"Oh, Mother, I'm so sorry. What happened to Father? Did he have a heart attack?" Samantha was pleading for some answers.

"Samantha, your father said he had a meeting last night of some kind and went out. Last night about three in the morning, the police informed me that Marcus was found. He had fallen off the ledge over Journeyman's End. What was he doing there? The police took me to the hospital last night, and I had to identify him. Oh, Samantha, what has he done now? Why are these terrible things happening?"

Just as Samantha was going to answer, Jonathan lunged into the living room from the foyer. His eyes were only on Beatrice and arms stretched out to her. She stood up and embraced him, needing him. She buried her face in his chest, and they walked to the other side of the living room. Samantha and Katherine looked at each other. Samantha took Katherine far away from this scene and lead her to the other side of the house. Arm in arm, they wandered up the staircase that the servants used from the kitchen. Samantha silently led Katherine to the fourth door on the right and opened it.

Katherine's breath was taken away. She was looking at a little girl's room. There was a large canopy bed in the middle of the room with starch white lace on top and bedspread, white lace lampshades with all the Wedgwood blue trim. There were blue tiebacks for the white eyelid curtains that surrounded the room on three walls, the largest windows Katherine had ever seen in a bedroom. "Imagine growing up in this room?" she asked herself. She was dazed by all this. She had never known such comforts. All the dolls from different countries lined up across the pillows. What a room!

"Samantha, you grew up in this room? How wonderful!"

"Katherine, now that you're here, I never realized how alone I was. I used to cry myself to sleep in this wonderful bed from loneliness. I was never allowed to have friends up here. I am so happy that you came into my life. I believe that we were meant to be together.

We will sort this mess out, and we will be together forever." She embraced Katherine with such contentment. Samantha whispered, "I really love you."

Katherine wept. "Me too."

There was a knock on the door, which shocked them both out of their tears. "Come in."

Jonathan entered. "The police are downstairs in the library with Mother. They would like all of us to join them, and I've sent most of the people home for now except the servants. Samantha, I am so sorry for all that pain I have caused you." He looked directly at her. They both took his arms and walked downstairs without speaking a word. There was such a complete sense of whole. No one could possibly explain what transferred among them. They didn't dare speak about it. Not now.

# Chapter 39

The three entered the library, and sure enough, the police were there. Beatrice sat in Marcus's wingback Louie the Thirteenth chair, and she signaled Samantha to sit in the other duplicate chair. To her surprise, there was a stranger among them. "Samantha, what is the meaning of bringing a friend with you? This is a family matter, and the police want a private conversation with us."

Samantha brought Katherine in front of her for her inspection. "Mother, you won't believe this. I was going to tell you later. Mary, my mother, neglected to tell Father something. That something was that she had twin girls."

Beatrice went white. The police officers didn't know what was being said. They didn't know why Beatrice was so flustered. She sat there with her hands twisting in her lap. Beatrice stared at Katherine wondering about all lies that laden this family. So many untruths. Yes, this woman in front of her was definitely Mary's daughter. Marcus was gone now and probably didn't know that there was another child born. Beatrice murmured, "I wonder what he would have done if he knew?" She smirked with a nod.

"Mother, I would like to introduce Katherine Donahue, my twin sister. I believe you knew our mother, Mary."

Beatrice got out of her chair and wrapped her arms around Katherine, never felt by Samantha. Beatrice had so many regrets.

She could feel the weight of the many years of silence replaced with self-pity. She was alone now. She needed everybody's support and friendship.

Like the clamoring of a bull, the chief investigator interrupted them and identified himself to all three. "When we have an accident of this kind, we have to be very thorough with all details. There seems to be some question as to why Mr. Rudolph was doing up there, and if so, was he with anybody? According to Mrs. Rudolph, she had no reason to believe something strange until we showed her something last night. We would like you to look at it, too. Do you mind?"

The chief investigator instructed one of the police officers to hold up the picture. Jonathan took the picture with both hands so as not to cover up the faces and names. They all looked at each other and saw that it was someone's funeral.

"Mr. Arpel, would you please be so kind as to read the names at the bottom and whose funeral it is."

"It seems to be Adolf and Adrian Rudolph's funeral. There are a group of people standing with a child sitting down in front. There is a man standing with his hands. Oh my god, it's Marcus. The young man standing is Marcus. No, wait a minute. It says that his name is Peterson, family friend of Marcus Rudolph, who is sitting down. What is the meaning of this? Samantha, what do you think?" He handed her the picture.

With disbelief, she looked at the picture and went blank. "This can't be true. It was definitely a stranger, Marcus Rudolph sitting in the chair and, Marcus's face, or Peterson's face, staring back."

"Mother, what is the meaning of this? You married him. Did you marry the wrong person? Who is he? Where is the real Marcus Rudolph? Did you marry the wrong person? How could you? Mother, answer me." Samantha was pointing to each person in the photo. "Who are these people?"

"Samantha, calm down." Katherine took hold of her sister, and the two of them sat down on the sofa. "The officer wants to tell you something. Officer."

"Last night we found your father up in the hills of Journeymen's End, where he fell over the cliff in the ravine. There wasn't any alcohol in his system. It seems to be my feelings and the other investigators that there was something strange going on up there. When we found your father, or whoever he is, he had this photo rolled up in his hand. That's what we would like to know and who was up there with him. I feel that this is a murder investigation. Do any of you have any ideas on this matter?"

Jonathan couldn't believe this, and Samantha was in shock. All these questions and no answers. What was her father doing up there? She held on to her sister and tried to work this out.

"Wait a minute," blurted Samantha. All heads turned to her, and the officer in charge shrugged his shoulders. "I was using an investigator to find my mother. Last week he went to Iowa City to find her. Instead, I found Katherine, my sister, on my own. When I spoke to his assistant, Paul, he asked me what did Mr. Phillips do with the picture? When I asked Mr. Phillips about the comment, he said that it had nothing to do with me and Paul shouldn't have bothered me with that. I wonder."

"When did this conversation take place?"

"Officer, I would say about 10:00 a.m. this morning."

"What is his name again? Did you say Phillips? Phone numbers? We'll be on our way, and am sorry to bother you at this time, but time is everything. Mrs. Rudolph, I am very sorry for the inconvenience, and we'll be in touch."

The officers exited, and then there was such silence. What did all this mean? The silence was deafening. Jonathan was up making arrangements with the servants. What was going on here? They were going to have a wake and funeral services for a man who wasn't the real man. What was this family doing? Where was the real Marcus Rudolph?

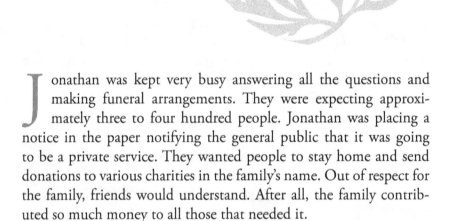

# Chapter 40

J onathan was kept very busy answering all the questions and making funeral arrangements. They were expecting approximately three to four hundred people. Jonathan was placing a notice in the paper notifying the general public that it was going to be a private service. They wanted people to stay home and send donations to various charities in the family's name. Out of respect for the family, friends would understand. After all, the family contributed so much money to all those that needed it.

Beatrice was lying down in her room resting with the help of the doctor's prescription. Her mind was drifting back to Marcus, whoever he was. He always did help others and was kind to those less fortunate. Why not, it wasn't all his money. He could afford to give it away because the well never ran dry. She was going to have to live with whatever Marcus did or didn't do.

When she was waiting for her new husband that day on the docks, something told her to run, and she didn't. She was so weak. Why couldn't she be stronger? Beatrice was reflecting back on her own sorrow and hoping that Jonathan and Samantha's marriage would withstand the test of time. "And if it doesn't, then she'll have to get out. Don't wait until it's too late. Who cares about scandals? Be happy. The family and our friends will understand, and if they don't, who cares? Oh, Marcus, why did you do this to me? I did love you. In my own way, I did love you, and now you're gone and I'm alone.

What will I do? I wonder what you were doing up there on the hill. Just think, Marcus, you had another daughter, and you didn't know. I can't believe it. Mary got away with something and played a dirty trick on you. Katherine's very nice. Much taller than Samantha and much prettier. I can't imagine what kind of life she lived back in Iowa. I know now that Father had something to do with her disappearance. I know that Samantha and Katherine will become best of friends. Well, Marcus, I can't think anymore. My mind is a fog. Two days from now is your funeral, and I hope somewhere you find your peace." She drifted in and out of sleep. Oh, that wonderful thing called sleep. "I wish I could sleep forever."

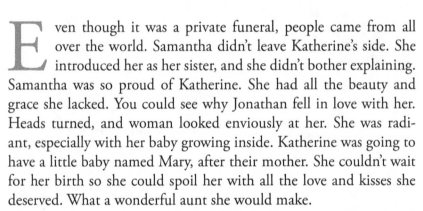

# Chapter 41

Even though it was a private funeral, people came from all over the world. Samantha didn't leave Katherine's side. She introduced her as her sister, and she didn't bother explaining. Samantha was so proud of Katherine. She had all the beauty and grace she lacked. You could see why Jonathan fell in love with her. Heads turned, and woman looked enviously at her. She was radiant, especially with her baby growing inside. Katherine was going to have a little baby named Mary, after their mother. She couldn't wait for her birth so she could spoil her with all the love and kisses she deserved. What a wonderful aunt she would make.

Jonathan made sure all the funeral plans were followed and limos were available to all. People were streaming in from everywhere. Since the wake two days prior, Jonathan was in charge of everything. The house was full of flowers, and the overflow was out on the porch. Beatrice told Jonathan that even with all these flowers, the house grew ugly. Ugly with lies and ugly with deception. She had to find out what happened.

Beatrice was in her black dress she wore for her father's funeral. Black hat, veil, and gloves. She was now going to her husband's funeral with her children. They were going to pay their respects to this man. Who was he? She still could not figure out why he was up in the hills. The long line of limousines was quite extensive. Rain started falling on this already-gray day, and the wind was whipping up the tops of trees. Almost the same wind blowing her away at the docks that day. It seemed like forever to get to the cemetery and home again. She only wanted to go home, slide down under the covers, and bury her head. She just buried her husband, and she didn't even know who he was. Every time she came to grasp the idea that Marcus wasn't Marcus, she could hate herself. What kind of a man would engage in such deception? But, she couldn't have known. She was driving herself crazy. "Oh god, please let everyone go home and leave me in my shame. I can't stand it anymore."

Jonathan was doing the best he could. People came back to the house, and condolences came in from around the world. Telegrams and wires sending sympathy and well wishes. He, too, like the rest of the family, was really in shock over Marcus's death.

Katherine finally went to rest in Samantha's old room. She was grateful for the large bed, placing all those beautiful dolls around her. What solace she felt being in her sister's bed. All the pressures of the day and past days came to unfold, and she definitely needed to rest. Her head was pounding, and she was having some blurred vision. She paid no attention to it and didn't tell anyone. She drifted off into sleep for a while.

As cold and damp as it was, Samantha beckoned Jonathan out onto the back patio, leading him to the greenhouse. He followed her, and when they were inside, she started.

"Jonathan, so much has happened between us, and I don't know where to begin. I can't blame you for falling in love with Katherine. I love her too. She's my sister, and somehow, out of this mess, we will help her get through this. I don't know what is going to become of us, us as a couple. All I do know is that I still love you very much and I want to stay married. So much has happened, and I need some time to think about what's in store for us. How do you feel about this?" Samantha wasn't going to stay in a marriage without the love of her man. She saw it with her mother.

Jonathan took both her hands with his and placed them on his chest, drawing her very close.

"I never wanted to hurt you, Sam, I have always loved you. I was drawn to Katherine and fell in love. It was almost like falling in love with both of you without knowing why. I must have seen you in her and didn't realize. Because of this crazy phenomenon, you and your sister have found each other. I don't know why this happened. Maybe she possessed what you didn't, and you the same. I love you, Samantha. I always will love you. Katherine is having my baby. Why is she having our baby? The baby you never seemed to want to have with me? Samantha, why is she having our baby?"

"I don't know why, and I can't answer that right now. Maybe because I wasn't a happy child myself and I didn't want any. All I do know, is that we need some time to think about what's going on here. Thank you for helping Mother out. You've been wonderful with all the arrangements and directions." At this moment in time, it was enough that they were in each other's arms trying to find answers.

"Excuse me, Samantha, Jonathan, but Detective O'Shea is waiting for you in the library." James, the butler, had brought a jacket out to Samantha, where she threw it over her shoulders. It was only about ten yards back to the house, but it was definitely needed at this late hour of the day.

"James, please make sure that no one disturbs Mother."

Too late, Beatrice was downstairs in the library with Detective O'Shea. Katherine was sitting to her right handing her some tea, and two police officers were near the back of the room. Detective O'Shea pointed to the chair where Samantha was directed to sit, and Jonathan stood next to him after shaking his hands.

"I must apologize for coming now, but I have some incredible news that can't wait. Samantha, the other day you said that Mr. Phillips's assistant mentioned a picture, and we followed that information up. After many hours of questioning Mr. Phillips, we learned some information and believe that he had a lot to do with Marcus's death. In fact, we believe that he murdered him for money. For blackmail. You see, Mr. Phillips learned that the real Marcus Rudolph fell overboard while coming to the United States in a terrible storm. In the photo, you saw a young boy sitting down on a chair. That little boy was the real Marcus Rudolph at the funeral of his parents. The young man standing up was Douglas Peterson, a servant to the family. He had been with them for years and on assisting the young Marcus Rudolph after his parents died. His parents were involved with antiques and owned property all over Europe. The young boy had investments all over the world, including oil in the Middle East.

"Mr. Phillips claimed that he had a discussion with him and Marcus slipped and fell over the cliff. If that was so, then why didn't Phillips call the police for help? We checked out the tire tracks left up there in the dirt that night, and they fit Mr. Phillips's tires. We believe that he was up there to blackmail Marcus with this information. We are about to book him on murder charges of Marcus Rudolph. I wanted you to know before you learned about this from the news people. There isn't any way we can keep this out of the news. When we go to trial, the public will learn as to why he was up there and that the real Marcus Rudolph died many years ago. There's going to be a scandal. Do you all realize what is going to come out of all this? Are you ready? They are such news hounds. I'm sure that very soon, you will be getting badgered with calls. May I suggest that you make a public statement and clear up this for the press, and then ask them to leave you alone? Otherwise, they will never leave. The news will make all the wires around the world anyways. Samantha, is it true that he was doing some investigative work for you about finding your real mother? Samantha?"

Samantha sat there listening. Everything she knew was a lie. The man who was her father was a lie. Katherine's father was a lie. But poor Beatrice! "Yes, I hired him to find my mother, and in doing so, he must have found out about Father. It all fits."

She glanced over to Beatrice, who sat there and didn't move. Not one inch did she move. She looked like stone, all ash white with her black dress and white hair. She had just buried a stranger.

"Again, I have to apologize for this interruption. It was awful timing. I had to come over and personally tell you what our intentions were and how they would affect your family." Detective O'Shea saw that this information was about to crack the family. He had to leave and let them digest this mess.

Samantha flew over to Beatrice and sat on the other side from Katherine. "Are you all right, Mother?"

Jonathan stood in front of Beatrice and tried to make her acknowledge him. There was only an open, transfixed stare. They all looked at one another and knew that Mother was in trouble. Jonathan didn't need to wait. He ran to the living room to beckon the doctors. They all helped her upstairs to her room, where they left him with her.

Beatrice was buried in her own thoughts, and her children knew that this high-spirited lady had broken. Mother had cracked. She never moved or spoke ever again. They lost her forever.

Beatrice, daughter of Henry Von Burger, mentally died with her husband. She died of a broken heart. Beatrice Rudolph never spoke another word to anyone nor acknowledged her family since the day of her husband's funeral. At the age of sixty, her children visited daily, but she never knew it. She just lay there day after day in her bed. She never knew the love that was given to her through Samantha, her loving daughter. Her gentle touches upon her face and whispers in her ears were never heard. She never got to know her daughter's sister, Katherine, who visited her daily. Beatrice Rudolph died before her actual death. They all tried to brighten up the house with their presence, but the walls were too stripped of love. Too many years of deception lingered in the cracks and crevices of the timbers. The foundation was cracked, and no repairs were worth redoing. No matter how much cleansing of the walls, they were too drenched with lies. The family was one of the wealthiest in the city, but the wealth wasn't in money. Yes, they had their wealth. It was a wealth of deception. There was so much deception. No daily visits could ever erase the lies of two generations.

# Chapter 42

It had been six months watching Beatrice in her denial. Katherine and Samantha went daily together for feeding her and helping with the nurses. They tried to keep up on the house and making arrangements for the food to be purchased and cooked by the staff.

Samantha included Katherine in every decision. Samantha finally had a real friend. A sister she could share her feelings. Katherine spent many nights sleeping over Samantha's. Samantha didn't want to leave Katherine alone. Her hovering instincts needed to be with her every minute. She wanted to devour her every word, doting over her needs as she began to blossom into the expected mother. Samantha was gloating and feeling as if she was the mother. She was experiencing every moment with her and wanted to even go into delivery room. Samantha and Katherine didn't discuss the tumor at all. They believed that it was going away and a healthy attitude would cause it to disappear.

Occasionally, the doctor would call from the hospital checking up on the girls. Yes, girls. They both felt like little girls.

Katherine asked all the questions about the big house and fancy parties. In exchange, Samantha wanted to know everything about her mother and grandmother. They had to get to know each other in every way. After all, they were twins. They were comparing their thoughts and feelings about everything. Even comparing the first time they kissed a boy and how each reacted. They giggled way into the nights and talked incessantly during the days, each learning about each other and loving every minute. They had so much lost time to make up.

It took Jonathan a few weeks to get over the fact that Samantha was Katherine's twin sister. Why didn't he see any similarities? Was he so blinded by his own needs? He loved Samantha. What could he do to ever make this up to her? Would she ever take him back? She was so wonderful about this whole thing. He was so sorry for what he did. Jonathan had such regrets. He realized that Katherine filled different needs, but he desperately wanted his life with Samantha. He would do anything to get Samantha back. He felt so betrayed by Katherine. She took all the choices out of his hands. He loved Samantha but needed Katherine.

The pretrial hearings were taking place, and there had been a lot of publicity. Samantha was able to handle it with the help of Katherine. After all, she was the other half of Samantha and now felt complete. Strange as it might seem, Samantha felt so whole now. There was always something missing from her, and deep down she couldn't figure it out. She had been cheated of her childhood with her twin sister but was enjoying every minute now. Nothing was going to spoil it now.

# Chapter 43

Katherine was doing her exercises on the floor of Samantha's guestroom. Her stomach was quite extended, and she was feeling the baby kick all the time. Jonathan was the typical expectant father hovering over her every need, but Katherine knew that he belonged with Samantha. The three of them lived as family. The three of them loved each other.

Katherine was leaning over trying to get up when she felt a pain cross her head, leaving her dizzy for a second. Her hands started shaking, and she wanted to throw up. The pain hit again without warning.

Katherine screamed, "Samantha, where are you? Help me, Samantha!" Katherine was screaming while in a kneeling position holding on to her stomach. Her vision was disappearing, and she was afraid to stand up. Sweat was pouring off her as she crept along the floor trying to find her way out of the room. The pain was flashing across her head again. She didn't know how to keep it from hurting her. She decided to sit up and grab her head with both hands and started rocking back and forth. "Samantha, help me!"

Samantha was in her own greenhouse. She was fussing over her African violets. Her spirits were flying along with the classical music blaring from the radio. She was deep into the music when she jolted from her knees to her feet. Something was wrong. She felt something wrong.

"What's wrong?" Samantha shouted. No one was there.

Samantha was dazed and felt dizzy by the terror she felt. She knew something was wrong, and she yelled for Katherine. In her own head, she could hear her name being called. She didn't know whose voice it was. It wasn't Katherine's. She wasn't familiar with the accent. What kind of accent was it? Yes, it had a definite Irish accent.

She pole-vaulted herself over the four-foot rose beds and started running through the garden. Thank God the french doors were ajar. She didn't have to go around to the other side.

"Katherine, I'm coming. I'm coming. What's the matter? Where are you? I can't find you. Where are you? OK, I hear you." That voice. That accent was telling her where to find her sister. "I'm coming." She flew to her on the floor of the guestroom.

Katherine was locked in a fetal position holding onto her head. Her body was shaking, and her eyes were rolling back. "Please, God, help me."

Samantha left her side for only a second and grabbed the phone. She dialed 911 and screamed that she needed help. The operator was trying to get the right information from Samantha, but she was in too much of a panic. She shouted something about her sister having some kind of fit and needed help. Samantha was afraid to move Katherine, so she rubbed her head and cradled her with the other arm. Samantha was trying to calm her sister while struggling to stay calm herself. Samantha was covered in dirt from the greenhouse, and now some was on Katherine. "Oh my god, please help my sister. She needs you. Where is Jonathan? He should be here."

The ambulance arrived with full sirens on, and the men ran up the stairs after hearing Samantha's calling. They didn't know that the patient was pregnant. They asked the typical questions. Samantha interrupted them and told them about the brain tumor and the baby. They called the hospital on that information and informed them. "We are rushing in a patient stroking out. Get the delivery room ready. We probably will have to do a C-section. Hurry," he commanded. The other paramedics strapped Katherine onto a board and carried her out of the house. Samantha was trying to grab at her sister's hand, but they were moving too fast. Samantha was chasing after them and refused to leave her side in the ambulance. Samantha heard stroking out. What did that mean? Samantha went nuts. "What are you talking about?"

"Lady, I can't talk to you right now. Your sister needs our help right now. What did you say her name was, Katherine?" Samantha was crying and trying to take all this in. Stroking? What about the baby? Her tumor must have done something in there. Samantha sat there in the ambulance watching every move the men did. Watching her sister's every breath. "Oh god, where's Jonathan? We need you."

The ambulance pushed its way through the traffic and jerked to a halt in front of the emergency entrance. Doctors and nurses were there to assist. Samantha had to find a phone. She needed Jonathan there now. The doctor grabbed Samantha and told her to wait there and he promised to be back in just a minute or two. Samantha stopped a nurse and asked about a phone, and she helped Samantha. The nurse sat her down and told her that she would make the call. She knew that she had a hysterical person here. "What is the number?" Samantha couldn't remember. She shook her head and shrugged her shoulders.

"Dear, calm down and let me make this call for you. Who do you want to call and tell me the number?" It was her kindness that Samantha knew that she had to remember in order to get Jonathan.

"Jonathan Arpel, Worldwide Fabrications, 545-9119" There, she got it out and calmed down for just a second.

The nurse made the call and got connected. She handed the phone to Samantha.

"Jonathan, something happened to Katherine, and I'm in the emergency room with her. Please come right away." He hung up. "Where is that doctor that said he would be right back? They all lie." The room was filled with people with all kinds of ailments and wounds. Some bleeding profusely, and there they just sat. "I can't believe…Oh, the doctor, he finally came back." It was at least fifteen minutes.

"Samantha, I have Dr. Myers and Dr. Kent with Katherine, and things look very bad for her." Jonathan then appeared, and Samantha went to pieces all over again. He didn't remember driving there.

"What is going on, Doctor?"

The doctor took them both aside and started explaining her condition. "The tumor is the size of a grapefruit, ready to take her life. We have a baby that is a little premature, but we must deliver now. We have stabilized her, but she only wants to see you both before delivery. Hurry."

Jonathan followed with Samantha at his side. They were in disbelief about what was about to happen. They entered the delivery room after quickly donning on sterile gowns. They were standing around waiting for them. Waiting for what? The other staff in the room, turned their backs, allowing them some privacy.

Katherine stretched her arms out to Samantha with all her IVs attached. She extended the one hand to Samantha and placed it on Jonathan's.

"Now I know why God sent me to you. You are my twin sister, and we found each other." She glanced at Jonathan. "I know why we were supposed to have this baby." Samantha's heart was breaking, and Jonathan was arched over in pain. The three were trying to hold back what they already knew.

"Oh, please don't cry for me. We're going to have a baby, and you both must promise me that you both will raise her. I named her Mary Beatrice, and I bestow my life and love to both of you. Jonathan, you belong with Samantha. I know that your love for each other will last forever. My presence here was only for an instant. I love you both. I'm so glad that I had this chance to share." And with that, Katherine Donahoe, sister to Samantha Arpel, lover of Jonathan Arpel, took her last breath.

Within seconds, the surgeon was standing there in his greens, telling them to move aside. They did a C-section. As Jonathan stood back to watch his daughter being picked up from her mother, he heard the scream of life. There was Katherine, now in the hands of our Lord, and this beautiful girl was now in his hands. She was the most beautiful thing he had ever seen. So small and fragile. So pure with goodness. Jonathan handed Mary Beatrice to Samantha so the nurses could clean her. Samantha was in such shock. She couldn't move. She gazed down at Mary Beatrice, her sister's daughter, and wondered what could be more profound in life.

The answer, of course, was death. How could she experience both at the same time? The doctors insisted they both leave the delivery room. Katherine needed to be prepared. Samantha gently leaned over and whispered in Katherine's ear, "I heard Mary calling me in her Irish accent. I spoke to our mother."

Samantha was devastated. She only got to know her sister a short time, and now she was gone. "Oh god, Katherine's actually dead. I am responsible for this child. This little girl who will never know her mother. Does history have to play itself out again? No, this time I'll tell her all there is to tell. From the moment she can understand, I will tell her about her mother."

Jonathan took Samantha's hand, and each walked slowly to the chapel. They knew that they had a great gift and responsibility ahead of them. They both embraced each other like never before. They were going to try again. They were going to bring Mary Beatrice up with all their love they had. They needed her, and she needed them.

Destiny brought Katherine to the eastern shores, where her mother landed so many years ago. Destiny brought Katherine back to her mother's roots, where she found her sister. Each needing each other without either one of them knowing why.

Oh, there were reasons for their clandestine meeting at church that day. No one ever knows what reasons we hold for the tomorrows. We can only travel through this life and do the best we can. Katherine was at peace now. Samantha was with Jonathan Arpel, her husband, along with their beautiful baby girl, named Mary Beatrice.

There certainly was a reason for all this.

It wouldn't have mattered which road each chose to take in life. Katherine and Samantha, born as twins, were going to be recognized as one in their daughter, Mary Beatrice. The apple of her grandmother's Irish eyes.

**The End**

# *About the Author*

Harriet Feltman grew up in the outskirts of Boston, Massachusetts, with her two older brothers, who were always grabbing the limelight within the family. After graduating a two-year business college, she married and had two children. She enjoyed telling her children made-up funny stories and poetry to keep them occupied or to distract them from fighting. It mostly worked.

Her desire to write stories was always nagging at her, so one evening she sat down with a used computer and put her imagination to work. *Wealth of Deception* was written on that old computer. Five years later, it was completed.

Harriet is now a Florida resident and cherishes all the storytelling she told her children and now her grandchildren. She is looking forward to recreating some of the stories she told for her future children's series.

"You never know what the future will bring. Create something that you love, and it will never seem like work," said Harriet Feltman.

CPSIA information can be obtained
at www.ICGtesting.com
Printed in the USA
LVHW031453261120
672639LV00004B/337

9 781647 012663